1

WHEN I FIRST met Mr Samuel
Blackthorne, I had no idea who he
was or that one day our companion-
ship would result in somewhat of a
celebrity status for Mr Blackthorne and by association myself to an extent. Or that the scribblings in
my diary would one day become published articles
featuring the exploits of my friend and the goings-on
at 420 Market Street. Still I could not help but notice
from almost the instant I set eyes on him that he was
a singular and highly unique individual.

The year was 1887, and I had just arrived in San Francisco after nearly a decade abroad. My first task upon stepping onto dry land was to find a room to rent until I could secure gainful employment and make arrangements for more permanent quarters.

When I inquired as to where I might find lodgings, I was directed to a coffeehouse where they kept a list of rentals that were located in the neighbourhoods nearby.

I'm not a coffee drinker, warm milk being my libation of choice, but I decided to make the drinking establishment my first stop on my return to the city where I was born.

My name is Edward R. Smithfield, D.V.M., and the last time I had seen San Francisco was sixteen years earlier. I was twenty-four years old, and the ink had barely dried on my degree in veterinary medicine when I set out across the seas with the smell of adventure in my nose and a song in my heart.

In those days, the Navy would pay for any qualified individual to attend medical school in return for a twelve-year term of service upon graduation. I

THE · ADVENTURES · OF

SAMUEL BLACKTHORNE

BOOK ONE

THE CASE OF THE CAT WITH THE MISSING EAR

FROM THE
NOTEBOOKS
of EDWARD R. SMITHFIELD, D.V.M.

COLLECTED
& EDITED by

SCOTT EMERSON

Illustrated by
VIV MULLETT

POCKET
BOOKS

For Kahley and Rainey

First published in Great Britain in 2003 by Pocket Books,
an imprint of Simon & Schuster UK Ltd
Africa House, 64–78 Kingsway, London WC2B 6AH

Originally published in 2003 by Simon & Schuster Books for Young Readers,
an imprint of Simon & Schuster Children's Division, New York.

Text copyright © 2003 by Scott Emerson
Illustrations copyright © 2003 by Viv Mullett

Book design by Mark Siegel
The text for this book is set in Golden Cockerel.
The illustrations are rendered in pencil.

POCKET BOOKS and colophon are registered trademarks of
Simon & Schuster
A CIP catalogue record for this book is available from the British Library

ISBN 0743469119

Printed and bound in Great Britain by
Cox & Wyman Ltd, Reading, Berkshire

1 3 5 7 9 10 8 6 4 2

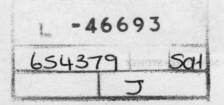

was able to take advantage of the exchange, and I felt privileged to be given the chance.

So when it became time for me to serve my country, I went with a feeling of duty and anticipation, as well as a light-hearted energy that has long since left me and I daresay won't soon be coming back.

But I'm getting off track. After all, this story isn't about me; it is about my friend and companion Mr Samuel Blackthorne and his peculiar qualities and characteristics. Specifically, it is about his incredible mind and his uncanny ability to see things other dogs couldn't and to smell things other dogs wouldn't.

His sharpened senses and highly focused intellect are not his only noticeably superior traits. He is very well read and seems to have an in-depth knowledge of an unimaginably wide range of subjects. From the inner workings of a Swiss timepiece, to the electrical impulses in the muscles of a frog, to the precise formula for the concoction of an extremely explosive substance made from the dried urine of the Peruvian fruit bat, there is seemingly no end to the diverse and arcane knowledge of the rather diminutive Blackthorne.

Although he has had very little formal education, he possesses such an obvious command of virtually any subject he chooses to discuss that all other dogs will immediately begin nodding their heads and making grunts and snorts in agreement with whatever he happens to be saying.

Blackthorne is small of size. He weighs a little less than six pounds, and yet he carries himself with a confidence and sense of purpose that leaves no doubt that he can be a formidable opponent no matter what the circumstances.

His family roots are originally from Yorkshire, England, and there's some evidence he is related to an unbroken line of terriers going back to the Dark Ages. Clearly he is of noble heritage.

When I first spied him, he was sitting on a stool near the front of the coffeehouse, staring silently into his demitasse cup of espresso with a look of sullen thoughtfulness. His dress consisted of a sprightly green tweed jacket, vermilion bow tie, and somewhat baggy khaki trousers.

Having just landed on the shores of this great country, and not having a single soul with whom to converse, I took up the empty seat beside him and ordered a large, warm milk with a dash of cinnamon and a bit of sugar.

The coffeehouse was a noisy, smoky place with dozens of patrons of all sizes and breeds leaning on the bar, sitting around tables, and gathering in groups, gesturing and talking in a variety of accents and at varying levels of intensity.

In one corner a Great Dane was towering over a table with cards spread around it in the obvious arrangement of a game usually known as three-card monte. Several others, including a Chihuahua, a

dachshund, and two Australian shepherds were holding wads of money and barking enthusiastically as the furry paws shuffled the deck and dealt out the cards with the practised skill of a professional gambler.

The bartender set my milk in front of me and I slid some coins across the polished mahogany of the countertop. I was just about to take a much-anticipated sip from my glass when a loud bark came from the direction of the card game.

"You, sir, are cheating and I demand satisfaction!" growled the dachshund to the Great Dane.

The room grew quiet as the crowd listened for the reply from the Dane. "Just exactly how was it that I was cheating?" came the low, measured answer.

"I don't know how you're doing it. I just know you are!"

The Great Dane slowly smiled and tilted his head towards the dachshund. "I assure you I was not misdealing in any way, but I can't very well allow myself to be accused of something that you aren't even sure I'm doing."

The huge dog looked around the room at the faces, all staring back at him. "Don't seem fair to let him lie about me like that, does it?"

Suddenly the depressed and downward-looking Yorkshire terrier next to me swivelled his head and in a clear voice addressed the crowd as a professor would address his freshman class.

"He's not lying."

"What did you say?" growled the Great Dane, for the first time showing a genuine menace in his voice.

"I said, he's not lying."

"How's that?" asked the Great Dane, his eyes narrowing.

"Simple," replied the Yorkshire, stroking his grey goatee. "As everyone knows, the object of the game is to bet on which of the three cards is the red queen.

"Now, our large friend here" – he indicated the Great Dane – "is called the tosser. He shows everyone the three cards, two black cards and a red queen. He then drops them face down and begins to move them around on the table very rapidly.

"The player tries to follow which card is the red queen. When the tosser stops, the player makes a bet and points to which card he thinks is the red queen."

The tiny terrier paused and took a sip of his espresso. The crowd remained quiet.

He cleared his throat before continuing. "If you noticed, the tosser held the black card in front of the red queen in his right paw and held the other black card in his left paw when he showed them to our German friend.

"That would mean that when he turned them over and dropped them face down onto the table, the red queen would be the card on top. That's the card everyone follows.

"Unfortunately for them, the tosser switched cards as he turned them over and threw the red queen down first. That means it was the card on the bottom, not the card on the top. Therefore, everyone was following the wrong card from the beginning."

The Great Dane smiled in an uncomfortable, nervous way. "My dear sir, you are fascinating us with your dramatic explanations. But how do you explain that at least two other gentlemen won more than forty dollars from me not five minutes before this bad sport lost a few pieces of silver?"

"Simple. They work for you. They're shills, fakes planted in the crowd to encourage others to play by making winning look easy. One of them is named Charlie Knuckles and the other, I believe, is Pepe Weddle. They're both small-time crooks apparently working for you, since neither of them is smart enough to win that kind of money in a game like this."

The Yorkshire chap turned back to the Dane, who now had a look of pure hatred on his face.

"So you see, my dishonest friend, your accuser isn't lying. Even though you weren't exactly cheating, you were definitely employing the use of a slight bit of trickery."

"Grab him!" yelled one old Labrador in the back.

Another barked, "Block the doors!" And before the cornered Dane could turn and run, the bar's patrons had taken hold of his legs and tail and were busily going through his pockets, removing cash and anything else they found.

When they had finished, they returned the

dachshund his money and then someone yelled, "Drinks for everyone!"

At that point the remaining money was slapped down on the bar, and in the ensuing confusion the Dane managed to escape with his life while everyone else pressed in to get a drink purchased at his expense.

"That was exceptional!" I shouted at the dapper fellow who had so easily seen through the gambler's tricks. "Let me buy you a drink, sir! That was one amazing piece of detection you managed there."

"Thank you, but that's not necessary," replied the blond-and-silver terrier. "It was rather simple, really. When I noticed they were playing three-card monte, I assumed the confidence man was playing the classic scratch-and-switch ploy on the unsuspecting German fellow. From there, things sort of took care of themselves."

"You mean you didn't actually see him misdealing the cards?" I asked in astonishment. "You were bluffing?"

"I made an educated guess," he replied, his eyes, recently dull and lifeless, now sparkling with enthusiasm.

"Weren't you afraid he might harm you for exposing him?"

He made a snorting sound and gave a sardonic smile. "Hardly a possibility in a roomful of gentlemen like yourself, my good sir. If, however, the Danish fellow did indeed decide to accost me physically, I believe I'm capable of dealing with him in a satisfactory manner."

At that moment, looking at the six-pound Yorkshire terrier with the green jacket and the smart red bow tie, I realised he was not only serious about winning a match with a dog twenty times his size, he might actually be capable of carrying out his apparent boasting.

"I see you've just arrived from the Orient," observed the sprightly gentlemen to my surprise. He then extended his paw and shook mine vigorously. "My name is Samuel Blackthorne. May I be the first to welcome you back to this country."

Apparently my mouth hung open as I stared for a moment without reply, because his smile grew, showing two small rows of sparkling white teeth beneath his neatly clipped goatee.

"I must confess I am astounded," I said, blinking in the amber light of the gas flame chandeliers. "However did you know I had just arrived in port not two hours ago?"

"That part is obvious," replied Blackthorne as he hopped back onto his barstool and picked up his cup of espresso. "I can also tell you that you have spent many years in the Navy, serving as a medical officer. Most recently you were stationed in Hong Kong, but you have also spent time in Panama and New Delhi many years ago."

My surprise apparently amused Mr Blackthorne, because he took a sip of espresso and continued his monologue with obvious relish. "Some time ago, you were injured in the left hindquarters, probably by a stray bullet, which has left you with a bit of arthritis that is aggravated by damp weather.

"You're a bachelor. You are slightly nearsighted and are looking for an apartment to live in on a temporary basis." He sighed and relaxed, his eyes glittering.

I waited until I was sure he was finished and thought carefully before replying, as if to verify that

I was in full control of my faculties and wasn't instead experiencing some sort of waking dream.

"I cannot believe you are able to guess so many amazingly accurate descriptions of me without employing the use of some sort of trickery or subterfuge."

I tried to divine the secret behind the small fox-like soothsayer. "Certainly you recognise me from a past acquaintance, which I have forgotten, and you possess an extremely acute memory."

"I have never met you before in my life, I assure you," he replied. "If you'll allow me to explain, I'm sure it will become clear that I'm merely using the powers of observation and deduction."

I removed the scarf from my neck, lifted my milk in a gesture of respect, and prompted Mr Samuel Blackthorne to continue his fascinating explanation.

He cleared his throat. "When you came into the bar, you were walking with the particular swaying gait of one who has only recently come off a ship from a long time at sea. I believe the condition is called 'sea legs'.

"I could deduce you had arrived from China because I happened to have just returned from the docks and witnessed the arrival of the USS *Leviathan*, a Navy ship on its return voyage from the east. Your cane is carved from cocobolo rosewood, which grows only in the Pacific regions of Central America, more particularly, the dry upland forests of Costa Rica, Nicaragua, and Panama. There is a Navy base in only one of those locations, and that is Panama.

"I know you are a medical officer because you have a tear in the right arm of your jacket that has been sewn together with a knot that would only be used by someone experienced in surgery. It is a double loop followed by a square knot. Known as a friction knot, it is more commonly referred to as a surgeon's knot. In addition, your pocket watch is a standard-issue Medical Corps chronometer.

"I can tell you were stationed in New Delhi by the silk of your shirt, a pattern that is rarely seen outside of India. I can also tell that you must have purchased it there several years ago, judging by the worn condition of the cuffs.

"Although you were exhibiting sea legs when you entered the bar, I also detected a slight limp when you put weight on your right hip. Being in the Navy, I'm sure you were exposed to some rifle fire, and I surmised that's what caused the injury. Since all injuries to such important joints as hips eventually cause arthritis, I made the further assumption that you would have developed that particular affliction.

"Everyone knows that dampness affects arthritic joints, and with you being in San Francisco, one of the most humid cities in the United States, I inferred the problem would more than likely bother you as well."

"How did you know I was a bachelor?" I inquired, still trying to imagine the precision with which his mind seemed to work.

"Your ring finger, of course. It's bare."

"And the nearsightedness? I'm not wearing my glasses."

"You have the small indentations on either side of your nose that come from wearing glasses for long periods of time. You read the menu on the bar without apparent difficulty so I knew it must not be reading glasses that made the impressions. On the other paw, if your vision were too seriously impaired, you wouldn't be able to navigate at all without your spectacles. Therefore, you must be only slightly nearsighted."

I tried to think of something to say but could not find the words to express my astonishment. "I am utterly dumfounded," I sputtered. "And the part about looking for a room to rent. How did you know that?"

"Again, it's simple. If you had family or friends to stay with, either they would have met you upon your arrival or you would have proceeded directly to their residence. Likewise, if you had an apartment of your own, you would be there now, rather than sitting here.

"Therefore, you will either need to spend the immediate future in hotels, which can be expensive – and on the salary of a retired Navy medical officer, you can scarcely afford many of those – or you must find other lodgings."

"You are again entirely correct," I confirmed. "I can't tell you how impressed I am."

"Why, thank you, doctor," smiled Blackthorne. "It is refreshing to converse with someone who has the intelligence and good nature to appreciate my verbal meanderings."

"On the contrary, Mr Blackthorne," I replied. "You are a truly fascinating individual and I'm fortunate to have run into you."

"Indeed, you might be more fortunate than you think." Blackthorne took another sip of the strong coffee. "You see, I too am looking for rooms and I've found quite a bargain, in an enviable location, but I need someone to share expenses or I don't suppose I'll be able to afford the rent."

"How much would my half add up to?" I inquired.

"Twelve dollars a month."

"That is slightly more than I wanted to spend, but if it's convenient, I'd be interested in taking a look. If it's all you say it is, I could probably afford it."

"Excellent," replied the Yorkshire gent by the name of Samuel Blackthorne. "Excellent."

2

LESS THAN AN HOUR later I found myself standing next to Blackthorne while he rapped at the door of Mrs P. F. Totts, a widow who ran a small kitchen serving breakfast and lunch.

Mrs Totts, who lived above the eatery, was also the owner of the building and was interested in renting out an additional set of rooms across the hallway from her own.

When the door opened, a rather large matron stepped out and squinted at our faces in the orange light of the gas lantern. She was an English bulldog and needless to say, she weighed in at somewhere between forty and fifty pounds. Her lower jaw jutted out so far she couldn't quite close her mouth all the way and her nose was pressed in to the extent that she snorted constantly.

She greeted my companion warmly. "Good evening, Mr Blackthorne."

"Good evening, Mrs Totts," he replied. "I hope we aren't disturbing you at this late hour."

"No, of course not, Mr Blackthorne. I see you've brought along someone to share the rent with."

"You are exactly right, Mrs Totts. May I introduce Dr Edward R. Smithfield, who has just arrived from many years in the Navy. We were fortunate to become acquainted, and we soon came to the conclusion that we might join forces to secure the fine apartment you are renting. We were interested in getting a look inside if it isn't too inconvenient."

"Be my guest," Mrs Totts responded. "Come in, come in. I'll just get the key and you two can take yourselves up there. I have my nightgown on, and I hadn't planned on leaving my rooms this evening."

"That would be most satisfactory, Mrs Totts," said Blackthorne. "I want to show my friend what an excellent location this would be, not only for its proximity to the best restaurants, but for the charm and warmth of its interior spaces as well."

"You had better watch out, Mr Blackthorne," she said as she handed him the key. "I'm liable to get a big head and raise the rent before you even get a chance to move in."

"Indeed, Mrs Totts," answered Blackthorne as the door closed.

Then, turning my direction, he said in a voice so quiet I could barely hear, "Mrs Totts is a wonderful individual, but I find it highly unlikely that her head could possibly get any bigger than it already is."

3

THE APARTMENT CONSISTED of a hallway with two adjoining bedrooms. A common bathroom with a shower could be reached from either bedroom, and the sitting room possessed a large front window that looked out onto an excellent view of Market Street and, farther on, the bay itself.

There was already a gently worn Persian rug on the floor and a stack of wood for the fireplace. In one corner was a large oak table with a good share of nicks and scratches in its recently polished surface.

Near the window were two slightly frayed but otherwise comfortable wingback chairs, and on the opposite wall, a love seat covered in velvet that had once been black but was now faded and shiny with age.

Between the chairs, a small oil lamp sat on a marble table. Two gaslights were mounted on either side of the fireplace, and their cut-glass covers sent shards of light bouncing at different angles throughout the room.

Altogether, it made for a rather pleasing effect, and I decided right then and there that it would make a spectacular place to live, even if the price was a trifle dear and the roommate was yet untested.

"You are obviously a man with good judgment," I remarked to Blackthorne. "It is every bit as comfortable as you described it to be, and if the offer still stands, I should be more than happy to accept."

"It's a deal, then." Blackthorne beamed, shaking my paw vigorously. "If I can offer any assistance with collecting and transporting your belongings from the docks, I am at your service."

"Thanks, Blackthorne, but I've just an old sea

chest, and I'm sure the coachman can help me get it onto the wagon."

"Nonsense! You've had a long trip, and besides, it's a crisp evening out and I need to get some air. We can stop by to let Mrs Totts know we'll be taking the rooms, and then we can fetch your luggage."

"It'll be nice to unpack my things," I remarked. "It's been a while since I've had a place I thought of as home."

"Then the sooner we get your things, the sooner you can move in."

"You, as well," I exclaimed. "I'm sure there are a few items of yours we need to pick up."

"Just a bag for this evening. I'll have the rest of my possessions brought over tomorrow from storage. We can stop by and grab the satchel on our return from the wharf."

Blackthorne closed the door and locked it with a satisfying click. We then stopped in front of Mrs Totts' door, knocked, and waited. From inside we could hear various snorting and sniffling sounds. The floorboards creaked as a faint shuffling sound came towards us.

"Who is it?"

"It is Mr Blackthorne and Dr Smithfield, madam. We have decided to take the apartment."

The door opened and Mrs Totts stood there in a maroon-and-gold robe with a black fabric scarf wound around the upper half of her head. It wasn't as large as a turban, but nevertheless had the effect of giving her sagging eyes and jowls a rather exotic flavour she might not have otherwise possessed.

"I'm so pleased," she remarked as she fumbled about behind the doorway until she produced a second key to the apartment. "Rent is due on the first, and I'll charge you a dollar a day if you're late.

"There are, let's see" – she counted on the digits of her black-and-white spotted paw – "twenty-two, twenty-three, twenty-four . . ." Her voice trailed off as she switched paws and continued counting.

"That's nine days left in the month, so I'll need" – she did some mental figuring, and her lower lip curled up almost to her black shiny nose – "six dollars plus a ten-dollar deposit that I'll give back if you leave the place clean when you decide to move out."

"Very well," said Blackthorne as he removed a

wallet from the back pocket of his khakis. "That seems like a fair deal. All right with you, Smithfield?"

I was already counting out my share. "Absolutely," I agreed. Then turning my attention to Mrs Totts, I bowed and handed her eight crisp bills. She placed the key in my paw and took Blackthorne's money as well.

"And there'll be no women or carousing, or I'll have to give you the boot."

"You can be confident, madam," I assured her, "that we will be prompt with our rent, and as for myself, I plan on living a quiet existence."

The huge head of Mrs Totts swivelled and her bulging eyes focused on Blackthorne.

"By all means," he agreed with just a hint of sarcasm. "By all means."

4

AS SOON AS Mrs Totts had gone back inside, we headed off for the wharf, which was only a short buggy ride away. We flagged down a large German shepherd pulling a two-seater and directed him to Pier 7.

I was enjoying myself considerably, and I let my nose fill with the smells of the city. It wasn't a particularly foggy night, but the closeness of the ocean gave the air a wet, salty taste that I have grown fond of in my many years in port cities.

I could smell the fish on the boats and in the restaurants. I could smell the mud of the shore. I could smell the blend of baking bread and kerosene lanterns and crates of spices arriving from the far corners of the earth.

"Invigorating, isn't it!" said Blackthorne, his eyes glittering as he watched the scattered groups of dogs out walking in the glow of the gas street lamps. "I love San Francisco at night. It's one of the finest nighttime cities in the world."

"I should say it is," I agreed. "I had the good fortune to see the city of Hong Kong at night. Magnificent. But somehow this is better."

"It is the city of your birth," said Blackthorne. "One always loves the city where one was born."

I could not remember when, or if, I had told Blackthorne I was born here. But I was getting used to his seeming ability to know just about everything about everything, so I didn't give it much thought.

He leaned over the side of the buggy and squinted as the wind ruffled his blond-and-grey fur. "It reminds me of Istanbul. I don't know why. Maybe it's the constant smell of baking bread."

"I've missed the bread," I commented wistfully.

Blackthorne nodded. "They say the sourdough made here doesn't taste the same as anywhere else. Some say it's the combination of humidity, barometric pressure, temperature, and salt in the air. Others say it's the type of wheat they use. I'll have to do some research in that direction. Which do you think it is, Smithfield?"

"Which what?" I answered.

"Do you think it's the weather or the wheat that makes San Francisco sourdough bread unique?"

"I think it's the particular strain of bacteria in the culture."

"Exactly, Smithfield! The microbes in the dough somehow influence the taste in a most favourable manner. Of course your medical training allowed you to see the obvious conclusion well before it occurred to me. I am fortunate to have one of your keen intelligence as my housemate."

I felt genuine warmth for my newfound friend as I accepted his compliment with a smile.

We soon arrived at the docks, paid the German shepherd, and entered the warehouse where my chest was stacked among twenty or so odd pieces of luggage that had not yet been picked up.

The dockworker looked to be a poodle mix or some other curly haired variety. I started to hand him my claim check when he suddenly noticed my companion and completely forgot about me.

He grabbed Blackthorne's paw and shook it up and down three times before releasing it.

"Good evening, Mr Blackthorne. I haven't seen you in a few weeks. How have you been keeping yourself?"

"Just fine, Max. How are the children?"

"They're terrific! My oldest was just admitted to dental school."

"Would that be Master Steven?" asked Blackthorne.

"That it would, sir." The dockworker beamed.

"Give him my congratulations." Blackthorne

indicated the ticket I held in my paw. "But for now we must load Dr Smithfield's sea chest onto an appropriate vehicle."

"Right away," answered Max. He waved over another worker and the two of them set about transporting the chest outside to the street.

"Are you a friend of the family?" I asked Blackthorne, referring to the dockworker, who was now hefting my worldly belongings onto a wooden cart.

"In a way," replied Blackthorne. "I once got him out of a jam and he's always given me news of his children ever since. He's quite proud of them, as he should be."

Blackthorne didn't go into detail so I didn't ask. But I began to suspect there might be more to my small companion than appeared on the surface.

I could only hope there wasn't a sinister side that had yet to make an appearance.

5

OVER THE NEXT FEW WEEKS I spent a good deal of time around Mr Samuel Blackthorne. We settled into a daily life that became almost monotonous in its routine.

I usually awoke around seven to the smell of coffee and hotcakes coming from Mrs Totts' kitchen. After a shower, I would descend the stairs and take up a seat at the counter for my usual breakfast of oatmeal. Mrs Totts would always greet me with a large smile on her sagging jowls and a cup of warm cocoa in her paw.

After breakfast I would usually return to the apartment to read the morning newspaper and catch up on any letter writing or business matters that needed attending. Around ten o'clock I would hear Blackthorne beginning to stir in his bedroom and soon he would pad across the hallway to the bathroom. I would hear the shower running and, twenty minutes later, Blackthorne would emerge looking still tired but freshly combed and clean.

He would nod in my direction, select from one of three different hats, and make his way to Mrs Totts' kitchen for several cups of black coffee and dry toast.

Although he was polite in the mornings, Blackthorne wasn't much for conversation.

Right about the time he would go down to Mrs Totts' kitchen I would usually begin my daily errands. Although I was planning to take a few weeks off before beginning the search for employment, lack of work made me restless, and I began to take long walks to various parts of the city.

Sometimes I would spend hours exploring different neighbourhoods and districts. I often got lost for short periods of time. But before long, I was travelling the streets with confidence and feeling quite satisfied with myself.

As for Blackthorne, his habit was to return to the rooms after breakfast and delve into one or more of the thick stacks of books, magazines, newspapers, scientific and medical journals, racing forms, files, and photographs he kept on hand.

He read incessantly, making trips to the library sometimes two or three times a week and coming home with an armload each time.

The mail bulged with his subscriptions. Messengers would deliver neat packages in brown paper with string around them. Blackthorne would sign for the parcels and immediately open them and begin poring over the pages.

The subject matter was diverse to say the least. There were books on foreign currency and textile manufacture. There were newsletters on business and law. He read newspapers from cities all over the United States, and several from other parts of the world. I counted at least seven different languages. But Blackthorne read them all.

He read magazines about insects, natural history,

botany, chemistry, industrial mechanics – the list was endless.

Each day, when he had finished reading, he would walk to his club, where he would lunch by himself until four-thirty. On most evenings he would then disappear until around ten when he would return and sit by the fire well into the late hours.

Often I would awaken during the night to hear him poking at the fire or scratching in a notebook while seated at the large table in the corner.

He kept a miniature Japanese pine tree in a small container. The soil and roots were covered with black volcanic sand and Blackthorne would water the tiny tree carefully so as not to disturb the neatly groomed texture of its surface. He had a pair of stainless steel clippers, small enough to fit in his undersized paw, which he used to trim bits of the delicate branches here or there.

He called it a bonsai tree. He said it was more than one hundred years old and had been in his family for generations. It had been a gift from his mother, who had died years earlier.

I waited for Blackthorne to tell me how he made

his income, but he never did and I began to assume that he was living off investments or family money.

Although I myself came from a less than wealthy background, I didn't hold it against someone who had inherited his money and therefore did not have to work for a living. After all, Blackthorne did appear to spend his time in constructive behaviour. He was obviously trying to expand his education, even if it was in a haphazard, disorganised way.

But I soon learned that he had no land or possessions other than the ones contained in our apartment. He earned his money by his wits, and he had no shortage of customers.

For the first few weeks, he had no visitors and I thought he was probably as friendless as I was in the crowded city. But on the third week he had four different individuals knock at the door, the last one returning two additional times in the same evening.

At these times, I would retire to my bedroom so as not to disturb Blackthorne and his guest, and after one especially busy evening, he apologised for the constant visitors.

"Think nothing of it," I responded, though in

actuality I was beginning to wonder what all the discussions were about.

"It's just that I have no better place to meet with my clients than the sitting room of our apartment. I hate to continually interrupt you."

"It's not a bother," I assured Blackthorne. "I am curious, though." I hesitated.

"About what kind of clients they are?" He finished my question.

"Something like that."

"I have a talent for finding solutions to puzzling situations," explained Blackthorne. "Dogs come to me with particularly confounding circumstances and I help sort them out. I charge a fee based on the difficulty of the problem and the time it takes to reach a satisfactory conclusion."

"You're a private investigator?" I asked.

"Not really," answered Blackthorne. "I call myself a consulting detective. Most of the time I can solve the conundrum without ever having to leave our quarters. I simply apply the science of deduction to the facts until there remains only one single, undeniable answer."

The Case of the Cat with the Missing Ear

"And you get paid for this?" I was still having trouble believing that, although obviously intelligent, Blackthorne could make a living solely from the computing power of his brain.

"Sometimes, of course, I must become involved in the collection of evidence. Often I must follow the threads of a case through a series of twists and turns before I can be absolutely positive of the solution, but I am never wrong."

"Those are boastful words," I could not help but point out.

"Not if I am simply stating a fact," he calmly replied. "Nevertheless, that is beside the point. I brought all of this up because I am uncomfortable with you feeling that you have to leave the room every time someone comes to call.

"Most of my business would no doubt bore you, Smithfield, but please stay if you like. You are certainly no bother and you may find that every now and then someone brings a tale of slight interest. It would be rare indeed that a client would object to your presence. Most are hardened professionals, police officers and such who care little for delicacy.

Furthermore, with your credentials and my endorsement, they'll probably heed your input with enthusiasm. If the improbable, however, does arise, and I feel you should leave the room, I'll give you the wink. How about it?"

"I accept," I answered. "I *have* been a little curious. But at the first hint that I'm not wanted, please don't hesitate to let me know and I'll make myself scarce."

"You have my word, Smithfield," he agreed.

One evening there was a knock at the door, and when I opened it, there stood a young lass with the sleek features of a greyhound.

"Mr Blackthorne?" she asked.

"No, I'm sorry to say." I bowed slightly and made a gesture of invitation. "But if you'd like to come in, I'm sure Mr Blackthorne would be happy to speak with you."

She walked in with an elegant gait and I ushered her to the sitting room. Blackthorne was reading a newspaper written in some sort of Asian characters. I alerted him to her presence, whereupon he stood and greeted the lovely creature with a gracious bow.

He then indicated me with a sweep of his forepaw. "May I also introduce my friend and colleague, Dr Edward Smithfield."

She looked my direction, nodded nervously, and sat down.

"Please tell us what we can do," said Blackthorne. "Take your time."

Her slender features looked wistful for a moment, then she let out a small sigh and spoke in a halting voice. "My name is Molly Kirkpatrick. I think something may have happened to my brother, Patrick. He didn't come home last night, and when I checked his work, they said he hadn't shown up there, either. It's not like him to stay out late without telling me his whereabouts, and he would never do

anything that might cause him to lose his job."

"What does he look like?" asked Blackthorne.

"Like me," she answered. "His hair is slightly darker and he has some white spots on his face and forelegs, but his height and weight are about the same as mine."

"Does he have any kind of a drinking or gambling problem?"

"No, nothing like that," she answered. "He's never done a bad thing in his life. I just know something horrible has happened to him."

"Where does he live?"

"With me. We share a place in the Mission district."

"Is that the last place you saw him?"

"Yes. We had dinner together the night before last. He said he was going out to get a newspaper and catch up on the local gossip at the pub."

"Did he tell you which pub he was going to?"

"No, he didn't, but he usually frequents a neighbourhood establishment known as the Pig's Gullet. I assume that's where he was headed."

"So he just never came home?"

"I'm not exactly sure," she answered. "I went to bed around ten, and when I woke the next morning, I assumed he had risen early and left for work without disturbing me. It wasn't until I got home that evening and prepared dinner that I began to worry. He never arrives later than six P.M. and at seven I decided to walk over to his office to see what was keeping him.

"When I got there, everyone had left except for the janitor, who told me he had not seen Patrick. He pointed out that he rarely saw anyone because of the fact that he began his cleaning duties after everyone had left for the day. But he did mention that Patrick's wastebasket was empty and his coffee cup didn't appear to have been used.

"I stopped off at the apartment of one of his co-workers after leaving his office, and he told me that Patrick had not shown up for work at all that day.

"That's when I notified the police. They acted as if I was being overly worried and instructed me to return home and stop bothering them. When I persisted, they explained that without obvious evidence that a crime has been committed, they don't investigate unless someone has been missing for at least forty-eight hours."

Blackthorne sat listening to the story with his elbows on his knees and his chin propped on his forepaws. Every so often, he would nod in sympathy or slowly close his eyes in thought.

Miss Kirkpatrick continued. "Well, I didn't know what to do so I left the police station and went to the Pig's Gullet where I asked the bartender if he'd seen Patrick the night before. He said Patrick was there and that he'd spent a quiet evening reading and talking with a few of the other regulars before leaving just after ten. The bartender said he left alone and made a remark about being tired on his way out. He got the idea that Patrick was on his way home to go to bed."

"Is that when you returned to the police station?" asked Blackthorne.

"Well, yes," answered Miss Kirkpatrick. "I couldn't think of what else to do, and I just knew he was in some sort of trouble."

"And that's when they sent you to me?"

"Yes," answered the young lass.

Blackthorne took in a deep breath through his snout and clapped his paws on his knees. "Well then, I suppose we'll have to see if we can turn up a fresh scent."

He addressed the beautiful female, who had become upset while telling her tale. "You should be commended, my dear, on your excellent detective work and attention to detail. If only our police force possessed your diligence, we might sleep a little more comfortably in our beds." He sighed again. "Ah, but it's hard to fault them. They do their best with limited time, funds and intelligence. At least they had the presence of mind to recommend my services."

"They seemed to be rather sarcastic about it, sir. As if you were some sort of mystic or something."

Blackthorne smiled and made a low grunt in the back of his throat. "I assure you, my dear, I am no mystic. Many of the so-called detectives consider me to be an amateur or charlatan, meddling in their affairs. Dogs can often be hostile to concepts or ideas that they don't understand. Envy and jealousy might also be somewhat to blame in their low opinion of my techniques."

"Well, I don't care how you do it. If you can help me find my brother, I would be forever grateful. Just tell me your fee and I will give you whatever the amount if you can begin your task immediately."

Blackthorne extended his paw in a gesture of dismissal. "First of all, I don't accept any fees until I bring a case to a satisfactory conclusion. And secondly, I charge according to how much time I spend and the degree of difficulty, both of which have yet to be determined."

The look of worry seemed to soften. "Thank you, Mr Blackthorne."

Blackthorne's face changed from its solemn expression to one of hopeful enthusiasm. "You mentioned your brother shared a house with you."

The young greyhound nodded.

"Could you take us there now?"

"Of course," she answered.

Blackthorne's head snapped in my direction. "Get your coat and hat, Smithfield. We've a lost dog to find!"

6

MISS KIRKPATRICK'S house was a single-story, Spanish-style structure on Mission near Second Street. On the way over she had filled in details of her brother and his habits, his friends and acquaintances, and any other facts that Blackthorne felt were necessary as she responded to his rapid-fire questioning.

Patrick Kirkpatrick was a hard-working, good-natured, honest individual who was somewhat shy, but was active in his community. He was an accountant by trade, having earned a degree in business from a nearby university.

He wasn't a miser, but he saved his money and lived simply. He worked at the same accounting firm he had been with for five years, and he hoped to become a partner in the company one day. He didn't have a sweetheart but socialised on occasion, although not recently. He rarely drank and never smoked. He didn't gamble. He didn't even stay out late. He usually spent his Sundays at the public library.

In short, there was nothing to indicate why anyone would want to kidnap him.

The cab pulled up to the kerb and Blackthorne paid the driver while Miss Kirkpatrick and I got out. The house was made from stucco and brick with a roof of terra cotta tiles and a winding pavestone pathway to the front door.

The front garden was small but well manicured, with recently trimmed trees and bushes that were shaped into perfect spheres of identical size.

We went inside, and while Miss Kirkpatrick lit some lamps, Blackthorne began to survey the room. His nose twitched as he sniffed the air. His eyes darted from object to object.

He picked up a book on the table and turned its pages. He checked along the carpeting, near the wall.

When Miss Kirkpatrick had the lights all going, he moved into the missing brother's bedroom. For several long minutes, he stood inside the doorway, as if cataloging the placement of every item in the room.

Finally he proceeded to the small desk and examined its contents. He picked through some of the papers on its surface and opened the single flat drawer.

He walked to the bookshelf and scanned the titles and authors. Most of the subjects had to do with business and accounting, but some were more obscure. There were volumes on watch making, steam engines, electricity, and a large government manual describing the regulations and execution of the U.S. census. He had a book called *History of the Abacus* and another entitled *Modern Sewing Machine Design*. There were several textbooks with names like

Simple Number Theory and *The Mathematics of Gear Ratios.*

"Quite a collection of reading material," I said, feeling a bit awkward as I stood with Miss Kirkpatrick.

"Yes, he enjoys a lot of different things," she agreed. "His hobbies take up most of his free time. It seems lately that I don't get to talk to him like we used to. He'll eat dinner and then head back to his books and his diagrams.

"Sometimes he'll ask about my day and he'll listen and nod and seem genuinely interested in what I have to say. But I can tell that he isn't all there. His attention wanders at times. It's obvious he's thinking about something else."

Blackthorne spoke for the first time since entering the house. "You mentioned diagrams, Miss Kirkpatrick. Could you tell me what kind of diagrams?"

"Gears. Machine parts. Things like that."

"Did he look at designs made by others, or did he draw them himself?"

"Both. He'd work at that desk some nights. He kept his papers in the drawer there."

Blackthorne frowned at this and removed a large magnifying glass from the pocket of his green tweed jacket. He leaned close to the desk and scanned its surface. He then examined the floor in a back and forth pattern that eventually covered every square inch.

Several times he used a set of metal tweezers to pick up a bit of something or other too tiny for me to make out. Then, with the greatest of care, he would insert the specimen into a small glass vial kept sealed with a cork.

When he was done searching the carpet, he looked through the wardrobe and made a quick stop

in the bathroom. When he was all finished, his face became somber and he addressed Miss Kirkpatrick.

"I assure you, madam, that I will get to the bottom of this matter as quickly and efficiently as circumstances will allow. There is no more you can do at this point, so I advise you to go about your usual business and try not to worry any more than is necessary. We have more to do, and you most certainly are in need of some rest. I give you my word that we will notify you of any progress we make as soon as is possible. If you remain here, it will make it that much easier to contact you."

"But I feel so useless," said the elegant greyhound. "I'd feel better if I could help in some way."

"If anything should arise, I will be sure to enlist your assistance immediately," assured Blackthorne. "We'll be in touch tomorrow afternoon at the latest."

With that, we left the premises and began walking down the street. We were soon picked up by a cabbie sporting a scruffy beard, a dirty felt beret, and a long grey overcoat. He was a mix of backgrounds that appeared to include some giant schnauzer or poodle along with the markings and build of a Doberman.

"He looks like he could be your brother," whispered Blackthorne as the cabbie pulled his cart away from the kerb.

"He's at least five times my size," I whispered back. "And if he hears you, he might not be flattered by your comparison."

Blackthorne chuckled and smiled smugly to himself as he put his nose in the air and sniffed the night breeze.

Although the dog was much larger than I – all cabbies were large breeds, otherwise they couldn't pull the two- and sometimes four-seater buggies – he did resemble me in a coarse sort of way.

His fur was mainly black, and consistent in length and composition, whereas mine is made up of at least seven or eight different shades and textures. On my back and neck it's rather long and wiry, while around my ears and under my chest and forelegs it is smooth and soft. At various intervals on the rest of me are sprigs of brown and grey in various lengths except around my snout and eyebrows where I have tan markings like those of a rottweiler or Doberman. Unlike the cabbie, I am of small to medium size, weighing in at thirteen pounds, and my build is that of a terrier.

We sped down Second Street and turned left on Howard. It was beginning to rain and the street glistened in the orange gaslight. Blackthorne didn't say anything further for the entire trip. He seemed lost in thought. He sat in the buggy with his eyes focused on nothing, as if, for him, the outside world no longer existed.

I squinted against the occasional water droplet and tried to make sense of what I'd seen so far.

Patrick Kirkpatrick had disappeared without a trace and, aside from something Blackthorne had picked up with tweezers, it did not appear that there was clear evidence of any kind. His behaviour indicated no personal reasons why he might attract violence. His acquaintances were few and none seemed very colourful, much less dangerous. If Blackthorne knew the answers, he wasn't talking, and as hard as I tried, I could not come up with any kind of a theory that would explain the circumstances of the poor dog's disappearance.

I decided to quit worrying as to whether or not I would be able to help figure out the solution. It was obvious Blackthorne had things well in hand. Instead I chose to sit back and relax while he sorted through the evidence, processed the information, and arrived at a conclusion. I had no doubt he was ultimately going to solve the case. His obvious talent for this sort of thing, combined with his infectious confidence, made it almost impossible to imagine him failing.

Staring out into the San Francisco night, he seemed invincible.

We arrived at the Pig's Gullet, and I tipped our cabbie generously for his exceptional speed at delivering us to our destination. It was raining quite heavily by this time, and we quickly ducked inside before we became saturated.

The Pig's Gullet was not a large place, but it had a warm atmosphere and the food smelled good. We pulled up a place at the bar and ordered refreshments. I had my usual warm milk, and Blackthorne ordered espresso.

When the bartender returned with our drinks,

Blackthorne tipped him an extra five and asked him if he could talk for a minute.

"Sure, friend," answered the red speckled spaniel. "I can talk about anything you want for that kind of money."

Blackthorne dropped two sugar cubes into the tiny cup of black liquid and stirred it absentmindedly. His eyes swept the room in the usual methodical manner.

"We're looking for a fellow named Patrick Kirkpatrick."

The hunting dog took out a rag and began wiping the counter. He visibly stiffened.

"It's okay," assured Blackthorne. "His sister asked us to help find him. She told us she had spoken with you about it."

The bartender looked at Blackthorne for a moment. "Sorry about that, friend. Patrick's a good guy, and I wasn't sure if you might be cops or something."

Blackthorne was solemn. "I assure you we aren't out to do him any harm. We just want to help return him to his sister."

"He was here," said the bartender.

"Did he seem normal?" asked Blackthorne. "Was he nervous, or did he do anything unusual?"

"No," answered the Spaniel, shaking his head. "Can't think of anything."

"And you think he left around ten? Is that right?"

"I'm sure of that one," said the bartender. "I know because we both heard the mission bells and that's when Kirkpatrick got up to leave. Said he was tired."

"Did he leave with anyone?"

"Nope. I watched him walk out myself. Always leaves me a decent tip, he does. More than I can say for most of the hounds in this place."

"Did he speak with anyone other than you while he was here?"

"Oh, I suppose so. There are a few other regulars he usually talks to. Let me think. Bartholomew Tibbets was here." The bartender tapped his snout while he searched his memory. "I believe Ricky Gossett and Frosty White were here as well. I know he's friendly with them."

"Do you know where any of these fellows live?" asked Blackthorne.

"No," said the bartender. "I don't usually ask that sort of thing. I stick to what a dog drinks. Personal stuff stays personal, if you know what I mean."

"I understand perfectly." Blackthorne smiled. "You have already been more than helpful and I thank you very much." He slid the spaniel a business card across the counter. "If you think of anything, please get in touch with me."

"Sure thing," answered the bartender.

Blackthorne pursed his lips and stirred his coffee. "What do you think, Smithfield?" he asked suddenly.

"You didn't ask him too many questions," I answered, nodding in the direction of the retreating bartender.

"I don't mean him," said Blackthorne. "He appears to be telling the truth. It seems that whatever happened to our subject occurred after he left here. I mean Kirkpatrick. What do you think of his personality characteristics?"

"I don't know," I replied. "He doesn't sound like the sort that usually makes enemies."

Blackthorne nodded. "Especially the kind of enemies that might cause you to disappear."

"Then where's that leave us?"

"Either someone took Mr Kirkpatrick, or he left on his own."

"But why would he want to leave his sister, a nice home, and a good job without telling anyone?"

"An unlikely situation, I agree."

Blackthorne arched one eyebrow, and I could tell he was getting ready to begin one of his informative but often lengthy explanations. As he had been fairly close-mouthed up to now, I waited with anticipation for the information he was about to share.

He gathered his thoughts and began in an instructive voice.

"There are four possibilities. The first is that someone has kidnapped, killed, or made off with him for purposes unknown.

"The second is that he has gone somewhere by choice, for reasons that are also not yet apparent."

He picked up the tiny porcelain cup and made a slurping sound as he drank the hot espresso. He then carefully returned the cup to its saucer before continuing.

"The third possibility is that he is unable to make contact with his sister or place of business because he is physically or psychologically incapable of it, as in the case of an accident or illness. He could have an injury or amnesia, or he's gone insane."

I waited for Blackthorne to finish, but when he began to get the faraway look in his eyes, I spoke up. "What's the fourth?"

"The fourth what?" replied Blackthorne in a somewhat irritated manner, as if I had interrupted an important thought.

For someone of his obvious intelligence, Blackthorne often surprised me with his apparent ability to forget he was having a conversation right in the middle of it. At first, I was severely offended by his rude behaviour. But after a few times, I realised he had no idea he was doing it. It occurred to me that he was not always in control of his thought processes. Sometimes they ran away with him; if his agile mind found a thread of logic, he was powerless to resist its pull.

His brain seemed to draw resources from all

nonessential functions in order to focus them directly on whatever problem he was in the process of solving.

I reminded him of our unfinished conversation. "You said there were four possibilities that might explain Mr Kirkpatrick's disappearance."

He blinked once or twice and appeared to come out of his reverie. "Oh, right. Sorry about that. The fourth possibility would have to include either pure chance, such as a random crime perpetrated against Mr Kirkpatrick that has left him dead or unable to communicate, or . . ." He started to drift again, so I prompted him to finish.

"Or what?" I asked.

"Or whoever took Mr Kirkpatrick meant to take someone else."

7

WE FINISHED OUR DRINKS and stepped out onto the street in front of the Pig's Gullet. I started to signal to a cab when Blackthorne took my arm and began to walk down the street towards a group of young toughs that had congregated at the end of the block near a dark alleyway.

"Do you think this is wise?" I asked, unsure if I wanted to confront a pack of dodgy-looking characters who didn't look like they'd hesitate to rob us or harm us, or both.

"Why, of course it is, Smithfield," answered
Blackthorne with genuine sincerity. "If you want to
know what's going on in a neighbourhood, ask the
youngsters who live there. They always know."

"But they don't look like ordinary youngsters," I
commented, keeping my voice low as we approached.

"Nonsense, Smithfield. They're no different
from you at that age; they're just trying to survive
like the rest of us."

"I suppose you're right," I agreed, remembering
my youth at the orphanage.

The group of strays was scruffy and dirty, and
they shifted positions as we got closer. The larger,

older ones stood their ground while the smaller, younger ones spread out to the sides. Their eyes followed us with cold, predatory stares, and one or two began to emit low growls from deep in their throats.

They ranged in age from as young as four or five to the late teens and they came in all sizes. Blackthorne walked directly towards the dog at the centre and introduced himself.

"Good evening, gentlemen." He nodded to several of the young females in the pack. "And ladies."

The leader looked like an Argentinean mastiff, also known as a dogo Argentino. He was almost entirely white and must have weighed in at nearly a hundred pounds. Dogo Argentinos were originally from South America where they were known as jaguar hunters. This one was obviously not someone to be trifled with.

He stared at Blackthorne, then at me, sizing us up for a moment before replying.

"What d'ya want?"

"I'm looking for someone who knows the area and might help us find a lost greyhound. It seems he left the Pig's Gullet last night and never returned home."

"We don't know nothing," answered the huge dog.

"I think what you're trying to say is that you don't know *anything*," observed Blackthorne.

"You makin' fun o' me." The dog's eyes narrowed.

"Of course not," answered Blackthorne. "I'm just trying to get some information."

A border collie stepped forward out of some shadows. "I think you had better get out of here if you know what's good for you."

The Argentino sat back on his haunches, and sensing that this was the real leader, Blackthorne addressed the collie.

"My name is Samuel Blackthorne and I'm not with the police or any other official organisation. This is my comrade, Dr Edward Smithfield."

The collie's eyes flicked over to me, then locked back on to Blackthorne, who continued speaking.

"Since you fellows know the neighbourhood, I thought I might enlist your help in finding out what happened to our missing greyhound. I have been hired by his sister to find him, and I am prepared to pay for your services."

The collie stood unmoving for a few seconds,

obviously thinking about the offer, while the others in the pack rustled and fidgeted.

"How much is it worth?" asked the collie. Blackthorne produced a roll of bills and counted out five singles before returning the rest to his jacket pocket. "This would be for your efforts on our behalf, whether you find him or not. If you bring back any information that leads to his whereabouts, I'll give you another five."

"What's to keep us from just taking everything you've got right now?" asked the collie.

Blackthorne smiled. "If you were going to rob us, you would have already done so." Blackthorne extended the money towards the dog.

"Besides, there's more where that came from and I often need the help of someone with your obvious . . ." – he looked around at the rest of the raggedy pack – "resources."

Finally, the collie nodded at the Argentino, and the huge white dog stepped forward and took the money from Blackthorne.

"Excellent," said Blackthorne, producing a business card with his address on it. He handed the card to the Argentino and continued talking to the border collie.

"His name is Patrick Kirkpatrick, and as I mentioned, he spent the evening at the Pig's Gullet. He lives over on Mission Street, near Second, so it is likely that he was abducted somewhere between here and there. His colouring is primarily grey to silver with speckles around his forelegs and chest.

"If you find anything, please contact me at my residence. If I am not there, you may leave a message with the landlady, Mrs Totts, who runs a small café beneath our apartment."

"What if we get the information and you don't pay up?" asked the Argentino. The border collie let out a small sigh, as if irritated by the big dog's question.

"You have my card," said Blackthorne. "If I don't live up to my end of the deal, simply wait in one of the many dark alleys outside, and when I come home . . ." Blackthorne arched one eyebrow. "I'm sure you can think of something."

8

I WAS STILL TRYING to recover from my surprise and dismay at Blackthorne's utter disregard for our safety and his seemingly complete lack of fear and good judgment, when he waved down a taxi and directed the driver to take us to an address I did not recognise.

"I say, old man, the next time you decide to walk into a pack of ruffians, I would be most grateful if you would give me some warning beforehand."

"Whatever for?" asked Blackthorne as he stuck his snout in the air and let the wind blow through his tousled fur. "You weren't harmed in any way, and you have to admit, this evening has been far more interesting than staying at home reading magazine articles."

"That may be true," I replied. "But just because something is interesting doesn't mean it isn't dangerous."

"On the contrary," smiled Blackthorne. "Danger is precisely the ingredient that can turn a boring and tedious existence into an exciting adventure."

"My years in the Navy gave me just about all the danger I will need for quite some time," I answered. "My intention is to spend the next few years trying to avoid excitement as much as possible. Hopefully, with plenty of rest, peace, and quiet, I stand a chance of recovering from some of my more interesting experiences."

"Point taken," said Blackthorne. "In the future, I will make it a priority to inform you of any plans that might put you at risk of bodily harm."

"Thank you," I replied, satisfied that I had made myself clear.

A moment passed and neither of us spoke. The

wind had grown cooler, and I listened to the clatter of the taxi's wheels on the cobblestone pavement.

Blackthorne's voice interrupted my thoughts. "You realise, you were never in actual danger." He continued to gaze off into the distance.

"Don't tell me you could have defended us against a half dozen street fighters." I was becoming irritated at his stubbornness.

"I wouldn't have had to," he answered in his usual confident tone. "First of all, they are, for the most part, still youngsters. Just because they live on the street doesn't mean they are criminals.

"The fact that they are so young makes them, above all, curious. Even if they *did* have plans to assault us, they were obviously waiting to find out who we were and what we wanted before they did anything violent."

"And you knew all that just by looking at them?" I asked skeptically.

"I did," came the self-satisfied reply.

"Must you always be so sure of yourself?"

"Only when I'm right."

I shook my head and bit my tongue. *How can any-*

one be so exasperating? I thought to myself. But then again, he *was* right. And after all, I *had* had more fun in the past twelve hours than I could remember having in the previous twelve months.

I decided I could put up with Blackthorne's stubborn, arrogant personality when the alternative was the dull, sombre life I had been living for the past several years.

We rode in silence the rest of the way until the cabbie pulled up in front of a large brick structure in an industrial section of town. The building was old and the windows had been painted over long ago.

After paying the cabbie, Blackthorne produced a large brass key from his pocket and unlocked the ironclad door. Inside, the warehouse was dark and I could hear the scurrying of rats as they made their way into the nearest hiding place.

Blackthorne lit a kerosene lantern that was hanging from a hook beside the doorway. The soft light shone on a large room of crates and barrels stacked floor to ceiling and extending far back into the warehouse beyond the reach of the light cast by the small lantern.

We walked along an aisle between the kegs and boxes till we reached a stairway that ascended to a small loft near the rear of the huge room.

At the top, Blackthorne inserted another, smaller key into the lock of a wooden office door. The word PRIVATE was stenciled in gold lettering on the frosted glass of the window and the hinges made a low creaking sound as Blackthorne ushered me inside.

"What's this?" I inquired as the lantern illuminated rows of test tubes, Bunsen burners, rubber hoses, flasks, beakers, and a variety of jars and containers.

"It's my laboratory," answered Blackthorne as he found a match and ignited two gaslights that protruded from the wall above a small desk piled with papers and notebooks.

"I was able to assist the building's owner in a case of industrial espionage some years ago, and he allows me to use this loft for my researches."

"You didn't tell me you were a chemist," I said, examining the bottles of assorted chemicals and reagents.

"I find that a knowledge of elements and compounds can often help me in my work. For instance, did you know that the mud taken from Golden Gate Park differs dramatically from the mud near Hunter's Point? Or that a fire set with kerosene produces a different type of ash than one set with turpentine or alcohol?"

"Those questions have never occurred to me," I confessed. "Whatever reason would you have for even caring about such things?"

"Isn't it obvious?" replied Blackthorne. "For instance, let's say a murder occurs in Golden Gate Park and your prime suspect denies having been in that location for several weeks. An examination of the soles of his boots turns up an exact match of the type of soil that can only be found in precisely the area he claims *not* to have been.

"Another example might be a fire that consumes a warehouse that is insured for a large amount of money. The police suspect arson but have no way of proving it unless it can be shown that the fire was deliberately set by someone pouring an extremely flammable substance such as

kerosene or turpentine on the wooden beams, floors, and rafters of the destroyed building."

"Fascinating," I remarked. "But what does all this have to do with Patrick Kirkpatrick?"

"Ah," said Blackthorne. "Good question, Smith-field."

He then removed the small vial from a hidden pocket, and I recalled the experience of watching him crawl around on Kirkpatrick's floor with his large magnifying glass and his tiny set of tweezers.

He sat down on a stool in front of a microscope and proceeded to transfer what I could now see were hairs from the vial to a glass slide. He used an eyedropper to drip some fluid onto the slide and then carefully slid another thin piece of glass over the first.

He turned up the gaslights to maximum brightness and peered into the eyepiece of the microscope while turning the focusing mechanism back and forth.

He hummed to himself and tapped his chin whiskers, then got up from the stool and went over to a series of small wooden drawers along the far wall.

"In addition to my chemical investigations," he explained, "I also have an extensive collection of hair specimens from virtually every type of dog, cat, rat, bat, moose, horse, cow, and a number of other animals."

He opened one of the drawers and removed a long box containing hundreds of slides with tiny, precise labels indicating the type of hair preserved within the fragile glass panes.

He selected one of the slides and inserted it next to the existing slide beneath the lens of the microscope. After a quick comparison, he removed it and replaced it with another from the collection.

He continued to select and compare specimens as he talked.

"By identifying the hairs found at a scene, I can accurately identify the particular breed of dog, or any other animal, that has been at that location.

"Again, we can narrow down the list of suspects to a short selection of dogs, since we can provide a physical description merely by knowing what kind of hair was left at the scene."

I nodded with admiration at Blackthorne's unending ability to surprise me with his cleverness. "So if you find the hair of an English sheepdog at the scene, then you know you're looking for an English sheepdog and not a beagle or a Norwich terrier!"

"It's not one hundred percent accurate," cautioned Blackthorne. "But you get the idea."

"I certainly do," I agreed.

"And if I'm not mistaken," said Blackthorne, peering into the microscope, "we can narrow down our list of Mr Kirkpatrick's visitors to a dalmatian, a Sussex spaniel, a poodle, a weimaraner . . ." – Blackthorne looked up from the microscope – "and an orange-haired cat."

9

WE RETURNED HOME after 3:00 A.M. and although I fell into bed and quickly began to nod off, Blackthorne stayed awake in the living room.

When I awoke the next morning, he had since gone to bed. It was evident he had been up all night by the sink full of dirty coffee cups.

I had a slight headache from staying up half the night, and I wasn't thinking about anything but breakfast when a knock came at the door. I

answered it, and there stood the dogo Argentino from the night before and a pug I had never seen.

The Argentino was holding Blackthorne's business card. His wide, white head seemed to fill the doorway.

"Somebody saw your boy," he said without emotion.

"Excellent!" I said. "Come on inside and I'll get Blackthorne."

They stepped into the living room and I motioned for them to sit down. The dogo Argentino chose the love seat. He was much too big to fit in the chair.

I went to wake Blackthorne and knocked on his door, then listened for sounds from within. I waited a few seconds and knocked again but still no stirrings from inside.

I tried the knob and opened the door a few

inches to peer inside. I could see his bed, and when I saw there was no one in it, I opened the door all the way and found the room was empty.

Apparently Blackthorne had left before I got out of bed and was already checking out hunches and following leads.

I came back into the living room. The dogo Argentino was sitting uncomfortably in the love seat. The other dog was in the chair by the window, looking nervous. The Argentino looked up.

"I'm sorry," I said. "I thought he was here, but apparently he's already out on his errands."

The white dog grimaced with indecision.

"What were you going to tell him?" I asked. "I assure you, I will give him the news completely and accurately."

"What about the money?" asked the Argentino.

"If Mr Blackthorne promised a fee, you can be sure you'll have your money."

I wanted to make sure Blackthorne had a chance to decide if the information was accurate before handing over the money. I also needed to postpone any sort of financial transaction for the moment because I had spent every last dime traipsing about the city all night long.

"Okay," said the mastiff. "Your greyhound was shanghaied by some boys from Big Bill Powell's gang. They knocked him on the head at the corner of Mission and Beale."

"Where did they take him?"

"Don't know," answered the white dog.

"Who saw it? I'm sure Blackthorne will want to speak with him directly."

The Argentino looked at the other dog. "He saw it."

I tried to think of what Blackthorne would say. Time was of the essence, but I didn't know what to ask. Blackthorne would know exactly how to extract the right information, to spot that one critical fact that would unravel the knot and find Kirkpatrick quickly and efficiently.

"What ship did they take him to?" I asked the pug sitting on the worn velvet chair.

"I don't know," he answered with a nervous laugh. "We didn't know it was your friend or anything, we just thought it was another sailor getting, you know, recruited."

The boy was referring to the practise of shang-haiing, also known as snatching or crimping. The method usually involved getting dogs drunk or drugging them or knocking them on the head. They were then loaded aboard a ship bound for China or Australia or another faraway port. By the time they awoke, or were released from their cells or chains, they were far out to sea with no way back. They would then be told that they could either work as a sailor on the ship or jump off into the shark-filled water.

"How do you know this dog?" I struggled to remember the name. "Big Bill Powell."

"Seen him around. Everybody knows who he is. But it wasn't him. It was his boys. I don't know their names. But I know they're his boys."

I looked at the white dog. "Where can we find you if we need to speak to you?"

"Lick House," answered the Argentino. "It's one block over from our last meeting."

"I know the place," I said. "What if you're not there?"

"Talk to the waiter in the bar, his name's Timmy,

he's an otter hound, brown with some grey patches. Tell him you want to talk to Salvatore, that's me. He'll send somebody to find me."

I shook his paw. "Okay, thanks a lot. We'll see you later."

The pug went through the door at a run, and the white mastiff lumbered after him.

I was getting ready to close it behind them when the Argentino turned his head and stopped in the hallway.

"Bring money," was all he said.

I closed the door.

10

I LEFT A NOTE for Blackthorne and went down to Mrs Totts' kitchen to eat breakfast. As usual, she was bustling back and forth between the stovetop and her guests at the counter.

"Morning, Dr Smithfield!" She waved her free paw as she poured fresh coffee for a poodle and a beagle who were seated at one of the three small booths.

"Good morning, Mrs Totts," I replied, seating myself upon an empty stool at the counter nearest the window.

Mrs Totts finished up with the two gentlemen at the booth and scuttled over to the stove where she poured some milk into a saucepan and placed it over a burner.

"Your milk will be ready in a jiffy," she said, puffing with effort, as her sagging jowls stretched into a wide, infectious grin. "What'll you be having today? The usual? Or are you going to be adventurous and go with hot cakes, waffles, or a nice raspberry pastry?"

I had had enough adventure for the day, so I chose to remain with my usual morning oatmeal.

"Have you happened to see our friend Mr Blackthorne this morning?" I inquired.

"I absolutely have," she answered, automatically checking the diners' cups and picking up the empty plates in front of two of them. "He was up at the crack of dawn, he was. He wolfed down a couple of eggs and some dry toast and left before he even read his paper or had a second cup of coffee."

"Did he happen to say where he was going?"

"I was getting to that part." Mrs Totts rolled her bulging brown eyes with exaggerated annoyance. "Said to give you a message, he did. He said for you to meet him at the Bayview Racecourse for lunch at one P.M."

"Racecourse!" I exclaimed. "We've a kidnapping to deal with and Blackthorne wants to spend the day at the races!"

"Don't really know if he had plans for the rest of the day," said Mrs Totts absentmindedly. "Just said to meet 'im there for lunch."

"Thank you, Mrs Totts," I replied. "I am much obliged by your willingness to pass on Blackthorne's appointments. If either of us ever exceed your ability to tolerate our impositions, please don't hesitate to remind us of our manners."

"It's nothing," she said, wiping the counter with a red gingham kitchen towel. "I'm happy to do it. Besides, it keeps me at the centre of the activity."

Her big brown watery eyes looked first right, then left, and she leaned up close.

"It doesn't take a genius to know that you and Mr Blackthorne lead a more interesting life than the rest of us," she whispered and then winked in a knowing way.

"I'm not sure if I would include myself in that

category," I replied, "but it is certain that you are astute in your assumptions about Mr Blackthorne. In the few short weeks I have known him, I have come to the conclusion that he is, most definitely, one of the most interesting dogs I have ever met."

"That he is," agreed Mrs Totts. "That he is."

"I'm sure Mr Blackthorne will tell you all about his current project as soon as he has time." I looked at my watch and smiled at Mrs Totts. "I'd love to tell you myself, but I must be leaving shortly or I'll never make the racetrack in time for lunch."

"Very well then," she said. "Can you pass on a message to Mr Blackthorne?"

"Of course," I answered. "What would you like me to tell him?"

"A dog stopped by earlier to see him. Big fella. I told him Mr Blackthorne had already left for the day. He asked me to please tell Mr Blackthorne he was looking for him. Nice guy. Very polite."

"What was his name?" I asked.

"Called himself William Powell. He said Mr Blackthorne would know him by his nickname. Big Bill."

11

AT THE RACING PARK I found Blackthorne in the restaurant, sitting at a small table overlooking the track. I pulled up a chair next to him, and he looked up with the glint of excitement that only seemed to be present when he had a knotty problem to solve.

He was obviously happiest when he was working on a case. As I discovered over the course of our acquaintance, when he wasn't, he was an easy victim to a dark depression that could take hold of him at any minute.

"Sit down, my friend!" He motioned to the waiter who came over and handed me a menu. "I have so much to tell you!" His brown eyes sparkled above his small white teeth and his red bow tie.

"I too, have much to tell." I leaned forward and began to recite the message from the dogo Argentino and his pug witness.

"Hold on, Smithfield." Blackthorne held up his paw as if to signal me to stop talking. "I already know all about it."

"How?" I sputtered.

"I figured it out last night after you went to sleep. The answer was staring us right in the face the whole time. I mean where do dogs *usually* go when they disappear without a trace? They are usually shanghaied, that's where."

"But where did you go so early this morning?" I asked.

"I went down to the wharf to have a chat with Max. He asked around and it seems there are three ships that might contain Kirkpatrick. None of them are set to sail until the tide comes in this evening."

"How much time does that give us?"

Blackthorne removed his pocket watch and checked it. "It's one-thirty now. High tide will be around eleven-forty P.M. We have ten hours."

"Shouldn't we get going?" I couldn't believe his casual attitude when there was a poor innocent accountant being held prisoner on a ship due to set sail for the other side of the world.

"We have plenty of time, Smithfield. In order to get Mr Kirkpatrick off that ship, we are going to have to locate him first."

"Let's call the police!"

"Not so fast, Smithfield," Blackthorne cautioned. "Most police are honest, hardworking, ethical dogs, but some of them, especially down by the docks, are crooked. If we tell the wrong individuals, we stand a chance of alerting the kidnappers to our presence. They could move him before we get a chance to find him. Or worse, they might kill him and dump him over the side."

I thought for a moment, and the idea of poor Mr Kirkpatrick ending his existence as fish food further sobered my already distressed mood.

"What do you have in mind?"

The waiter brought our salads and drinks, and Blackthorne filled his mouth with a huge forkful of lettuce, chewing several times before continuing.

"I'll give you the details on that later. Needless to say, we will have to act under cover of night. Therefore we can spend an hour or two here at the park because we don't have to be anywhere till sundown."

"What about Miss Kirkpatrick?" I imagined the poor thing sitting at home, crying for her brother and hearing no word as to his whereabouts or condition.

"I've already spoken to her," said Blackthorne as he used his fork to stab an olive and a small yellow tomato. "She's aware that we're making some headway."

"You, my good man, are efficient," I observed with admiration. "But I do have one more piece of information that you may not want to hear."

"Let me guess," said Blackthorne. "Big Bill Powell came by to see me."

"Is there nothing you don't know? It seems you are some kind of sorcerer!" I was now fully flabbergasted

The Case of the Cat with the Missing Ear

The Case of the Cat with the Missing Ear

by Blackthorne's almost mystical talent for conjuring up information out of nothing. "Someone obviously has informed you of that fact before I was able to speak with you."

"No, that's not it, Smithfield." He chuckled to himself. "I knew Big Bill Powell came by to visit for the simple reason that I sent him an invitation."

12

12

"I HAVE BEEN WATCHING the workings of the race track since before you arrived," said Blackthorne, "and I find it utterly fascinating." I was finishing off the last of my meal, an excellent portion of salmon with a horseradish-mustard sauce, and my mouth was too full to comment.

Throughout lunch Blackthorne had filled me in on the details of the morning's activity. If there were any doubts remaining in my mind as to the intelligence, cunning, and sheer bravado of Mr Samuel

Blackthorne, I was thoroughly and completely relieved of them as he laid out his plans.

When he had finished, he changed the subject and began talking as if none of it had ever happened, and we were just two gentlemen out for a Sunday afternoon at the races.

"The odds, shown over there on the tote board" – he pointed at the huge black board on the far side of the track – "are determined by the likelihood of a particular dog winning the next race."

Small dogs walked back and forth on planks in

front of the black board. They were constantly changing the numbers shown beside the name of the next race's participants.

"Let's say the odds are two to one on the dog you think will win. That means that for every dollar you bet, you stand a chance to win two dollars if your dog comes in first."

"I understand the mechanics of gambling," I replied.

"Then make sure I am understanding it correctly," said Blackthorne, "because I don't want to miss anything important."

I nodded without saying anything. I wasn't sure if Blackthorne truly wanted my help or he was just humouring me.

"In any case," he continued, "if you are the only one who thinks a particular dog will win the race and everyone else bets on another dog, then your odds will be higher, like ten to one, for instance.

"If you bet on a dog at ten-to-one odds, then you stand a chance of winning *ten* dollars for every one you bet."

"I understand the concept," I said.

"Since the odds are determined by how much is bet on each individual dog, the figures would change constantly and rapidly. It must take a lot of adding and dividing to figure out all those numbers so quickly."

"I've never thought about it," I said, "but that's probably why they can't run more races. Even with forty minutes between start times, they have to count up all the bets and refigure the odds pretty fast to get them on the tote board in time."

Blackthorne's eyes swept the crowd in the bleachers on the level below ours. Although we were seated in the more expensive area of the racetrack, the majority of spectators sat down near the track where one did not have to buy lunch or dinner.

There were dogs packed shoulder-to-shoulder holding their betting receipts in their paws, shouting and barking at the dog of their choice to outrun the others. The race was set to begin in less than two minutes, and the participants were walking on the sidelines, warming up before getting into their starting positions.

"In addition to betting on which dog you think will win, you can bet on which dog takes second and third as well," said Blackthorne. "Then, if you're feeling particularly lucky, you can bet on which dogs you think will take both first and second place, in order. That is called an exacta. A quinella is the first and second place in any order, and a trifecta is all three finishers in order."

"Whatever happened to plain old betting on a single participant?" I sighed. "It's too complicated."

"It's all about getting as much of the gambler's money as possible," said Blackthorne. "The more the players bet, the more the track makes."

Blackthorne's eyes glazed over for a moment as they often did when he was busy thinking. When he once again returned to the present, he continued the conversation as if the break hadn't occurred at all.

"Can you imagine how much more cash the track could generate if they could figure the odds twice as fast? They could double the number of races."

His gleaming eyes flashed as another thought came to him.

"Right now, there are two other locations where you can bet on the races at this track from across town. A telegraph wire connects the casinos and adds in their money to the totals.

"The track could make even more if it had a window for placing bets in every saloon and hotel in town. All it would take would be more telegraph lines and a way to tally all the bets."

"Why all the talk about gambling?" I asked.

Blackthorne paused for a moment and pushed away a small cut-glass bowl of ice cream the waiter had set down in front of him.

"I've done some checking on Big Bill, and it seems that his primary business is gambling. In fact he just happens to own this very racetrack that we find ourselves enjoying so immensely."

13

W E LEFT THE TRACK and headed to Lick House, the hotel where the Argentino had told us to meet him. When we entered the building, we asked directions to the bar and found it to be pleasant, though on the dark side. We sat at a table near the front and ordered drinks. Blackthorne scanned the patrons, as did I. The white-haired mastiff was nowhere to be found.

When the waiter returned, Blackthorne paid for the espresso and milk and added a hefty tip. "Would you be Timmy?"

"I surely would," answered the grey-and-brown otter hound.

"We are looking for a friend of ours by the name of Salvatore. Would you know how we might get in touch with him?"

"I might," answered the waiter. "It might help my memory if you told me who's doing the asking."

"My name's Samuel Blackthorne, and this is my colleague, Dr Edward R. Smithfield. He told us to meet him here and ask for you if he wasn't immediately available."

"Okay, okay, I know who you are," said the otter hound. "I already sent somebody to go get him. I recognised you when you came in."

"Then why did you make us go through such a long-winded explanation?" I asked.

"I had to be sure, that's all. If Salvatore got here and you were cops or something, I'd be in trouble."

"I suppose you would," I conceded.

Blackthorne tipped young Timmy an extra dollar and we waited for Salvatore to arrive.

"How did you narrow it down to only three ships?" I asked Blackthorne, referring of course to the dozens of ships that came and went from the harbour of San Francisco Bay every day.

"First of all, I could eliminate any ships that were going on short trips up or down the coast. Only ships that are headed out to sea would want a sailor that has been shanghaied. Three of the ships were going to Alaska with more than one stop scheduled along the way.

"Second, the large ships don't participate in the practise, generally speaking. Big business frowns on any association with illegal activity. The same goes for Navy ships or anything having to do with the government.

"I narrowed the list down to seven and then went to visit my friend Max at the docks. He did some asking around and discovered that three of the seven had, in fact, received deliveries of what appeared to be unconscious crew members the night before.

"Only one of the three took a single body onboard. The others received *packages* of two or more."

"So you think the single, unconscious victim is our Mr Kirkpatrick?"

"I have no doubt."

Just then the dogo Argentino walked up to the table and pulled up a chair. It creaked as he sat down.

"Salvatore!" Blackthorne reached across and shook the mastiff's paw. "Thank you for arriving so quickly."

The white dog nodded but didn't speak.

"Won't you have a drink with us?" asked Blackthorne. "Coffee?"

"No, thanks," answered the Argentino.

Blackthorne pulled an envelope out of his breast pocket. "You'll find it's all there." He reached across the table and laid it in front of the scowling mastiff. "In fact, I doubled the amount we agreed on."

The white dog didn't pick up the envelope right away. "Why would you do a thing like that?"

"Because I would like your help," answered Blackthorne. "We have to get the kidnapped fellow off the ship and we can't do it alone."

"I don't think so," said the Argentino. "I'll just take the five."

"It's nothing dangerous, I assure you," said Blackthorne. "You won't be sneaking around in the dead of night or anything like that."

"If you're not conking somebody, why do you need us?"

"Not *us*," corrected Blackthorne. "You, Salvatore. We need you."

The big mastiff leaned back in his chair and looked down his nose at Blackthorne. "Why me?"

"You're big enough to carry our Mr Kirkpatrick. He's a bit much for someone of my build, and Dr Smithfield has a touch of arthritis that I would not want to aggravate in any way."

The big dog's face became even more serious as he weighed the estimated risk against the extra five-dollar payoff.

Blackthorne quietly added, "You can split the extra with your friends, or not, your choice. I will also include an additional five-dollar personal bonus if everything goes right."

The Argentino made up his mind. "All right, I'm in."

"Excellent," said Blackthorne.

"But I'm wondering something."

"Ask away."

"Why do I have to carry this guy? Why can't he just walk?"

"Isn't it obvious?" asked Blackthorne. "He'll be unconscious, of course."

14

THE SUN HAD SET around 6:30 P.M. and the fog was rolling in across the city. In San Francisco the fog doesn't come in off the bay. It rolls down from behind the city like a slow, thick, blue-grey waterfall, flowing into the bay from the west.

When the fog comes in, it changes everything. Visibility goes down to a few dozen yards or, if it's thick, a few dozen feet. Even the brightest lights become dim and faint. Smells are absorbed into the mist. It cleans the air like a giant sponge, washing away all the dust and smoke, all the grunge and grime that has built up during the day's activities.

But the most fascinating thing about the fog is that it absorbs and dampens all sound.

The clanking and clacking and arguing and ringing and yelling and whistling and barking and pounding and clattering that are usually heard near the docks in the city become quiet.

It is as if everything is farther away. The foghorn becomes a distant wail, a mournful beast calling to its mate. The ringing of bells becomes a faint tinkling. If you bark or shout, the sound doesn't bounce around or come back to you in an echo. It disappears, sucked up by the cold mist.

The ship, the *Cuthbert*, was tied up at Pier 13, gently bobbing in the black water. A large white dog came down the brick-paved roadway, pulling a small wagon with two occupants. They were wearing white cotton uniforms that bore the insignia of the city hospital on the lapels. They pulled up in front of the *Cuthbert* and got out.

"Hello there," shouted the smaller one to the ship. "Anybody aboard?"

A grizzled head popped up above the railings of the *Cuthbert*. "What d'ya want?"

"We need to speak to your medical officer."

The sea dog wore a gold nose ring, and one eye had the hazy whitish look of blindness. He laughed a wheezing, wet cackle. "We don't have no medical officer! And if you don't get outta here I'm going to come down there and give you a *real* need for medical attention!"

"Have you ever seen anyone with rabies?" asked the taller of the two dressed in white.

There was no sound from the ship for several seconds.

"I asked if you'd ever seen anyone with the disease rabies?"

"I heard you!" came the sudden reply. "What do ya mean? I mean why would you ask something like that?"

"Because you don't seem to understand the importance of our visit. You see, we are medical workers and we've received a report that one of your crew members may have contracted rabies."

"What's contracted?" asked the sea dog. By this time, there were three other heads looking over the side rail.

"*Contracted* means that he might have caught the disease," explained the smaller of the two health workers. "If you don't have a medical officer, we need to talk to the captain."

"He ain't here."

"Then who is in charge? If we don't examine this dog immediately, he could infect the whole ship!"

"Wait there a minute," instructed the old sailor. He disappeared for a moment, and when he reappeared, he had a golden retriever with him. The retriever surveyed the two medical workers, then spoke with a much higher, squeakier voice than one would expect from a dog of that size.

"May I help you?"

"Yes," answered the taller of the two on shore. "I believe you have a crew member by the name of Patrick Kirkpatrick on board the *Cuthbert*, and we need to examine him. There is an extremely strong likelihood that Mr Kirkpatrick has rabies."

"We don't have no one named Kirkpatrick on *this* ship," came the angry reply.

The voice of the health worker carried clear and strong, even in the fog. "If your crew member isn't treated, he will soon succumb to the effects of the disease and my good sir, you *do not* want that to happen."

"I told you, there ain't no one named Kirkpatrick onboard!"

"Are you sure?" shouted the health worker. "He's a greyhound, silver with speckles on his forelegs and chest."

The sea dog was silent.

"It is imperative that we examine him. If the disease is allowed to progress, he will suffer delusions. He may become violent. If he manages to get his teeth into someone, he would most certainly infect them as well."

"Get his teeth into someone?" repeated the high-pitched retriever.

"Most certainly," answered the white-coated medical worker. "Dogs with rabies have been said to have the strength of ten dogs. Once the fever takes hold, there's almost nothing to stop the violent rages of the victim.

"It's also called hydrophobia, which means fear of water. They call it that because even though you have a raging thirst, you can't bring yourself to drink. You foam at the mouth and howl from dusk till dawn."

The health worker went on. "Once I heard of a ship that left harbour with a crew of sixteen. A month later it was found floating at sea without a soul aboard."

He waited for the words to sink in before finishing. "They think it was rabies."

The retriever looked at the old sea dog. They both looked at the health workers and back at each other.

"I give you my word that we are only interested in the well-being of Mr Kirkpatrick and the remaining uninfected crew members of this ship." The health worker emphasised the word *uninfected*.

"How did you find out this guy was here?" asked the golden retriever. "I mean he's not, but you seem to be pretty sure of yourself."

"I don't know. We're just the case workers assigned to examine Mr Kirkpatrick."

"You sure you're not cops?"

"Do we look like cops?" asked the smallest of the pair.

"Not really," answered the squeaky retriever.

"Then let us aboard."

"I don't know what the captain 'ill say."

"What will he say if you let a diseased dog infect everyone aboard?"

The golden retriever hesitated, then snorted and shook his head. "I shouldn't be doing this."

"Come on, man!" shouted the health worker. "We haven't a second to waste!"

"Fine, come aboard! The guy's been nothing but trouble anyway."

The gangplank was extended, and the two white-coated officials quickly ascended the wooden ramp.

The retriever led them to a compartment belowdeck where he unlocked the door and ushered them inside. In one corner of the tiny room, in the shadows cast by the swinging lantern in the retriever's paw, there lay a greyhound curled up on the floor.

"There he is," said the big dog. "He's been sick all day."

"I hope we're not already too late," said the smaller of the two health officials. The other was already bent down, checking the pulse of the unconscious greyhound.

The eyelids were pulled back and the stethoscope was rapidly applied to the lungs.

"We must get him to a hospital immediately," announced the health worker as he stood and replaced the stethoscope into the black medical bag.

"Does he got it?" asked the scruffy, matted sea dog. "Does he got the sickness?"

"Can't you see?" exclaimed the smaller official. "There isn't a moment to lose!"

The health official pointed at two others of the ship's crew. "You there! And you! Get his legs and carry him onto shore!"

The command was barked with such sharpness, such confidence, that the two wide-eyed sailors acted without thinking. They picked up the limp greyhound and carried him down the gangplank to the wooden dock.

The third medical worker, a large white dog who had been waiting onshore, lifted the unconscious patient into the hospital wagon.

"You did the right thing," said the shorter of the two officials as he got into the cart. "If any of you start to feel funny, get to the hospital immediately."

"What do you mean funny?" shouted the retriever, but the wagon drove away. Within seconds it had disappeared into the fog.

Soon even the clatter of its wheels on the brick pavement was lost in the mist.

15

I SAY, BLACKTHORNE." I was still trying to catch my breath from laughing. "I haven't had that much fun since I was a pup!"

"It *was* quite amusing," he answered with a grin. "How's our patient?"

"He'll have a heck of a headache when he wakes up. But considering what he's been through, he seems fairly healthy to me. Of course, I will give him a thorough physical once we get him into a bed, but I think most of his problem is the result of the drugs he's been given. The night air seems to be helping him come around."

I couldn't believe that we had just succeeded in getting the sailors to hand him over so easily. We were now barrelling down the cobbled streets towards Molly Kirkpatrick's house with her groggy but otherwise unharmed brother and the case solved.

"You have quite an air of command about you," shouted Blackthorne over the clatter of the wheels.

"That comes from being a doctor," I yelled back. "You aren't so bad yourself! You had that golden retriever so scared he couldn't think straight."

"I'd hate to be in their boots when the captain gets back. We were lucky he wasn't there. He might not have been so easily fooled."

"Lucky they didn't know much about rabies!"

"I'm sure you would have thought of something," said Blackthorne.

I made an exaggerated bow and nearly fell off the cart as the big Argentino made a sharp corner.

I pulled myself back in just as the greyhound opened his bloodshot eyes. He tried to raise his head but gave up and instead looked around at the passing scenery from a reclining position.

"He's had enough chloroform to keep him drugged for days. I'm impressed that he's even awake."

"If he's anything like his sister," observed Blackthorne, "he's an exceptional physical specimen."

"I'll go along with that opinion," I agreed.

"I had no doubt you would," said Blackthorne.

16

WE DROPPED OFF the semiconscious greyhound at his house and left him in his sister's capable care. She was overjoyed to see him, of course, and asked us to stay for dinner while he slept. I was opening my mouth to accept the invitation when Blackthorne interrupted me to apologise and say that we were, "unfortunately, expected elsewhere for a prior engagement."

Miss Kirkpatrick seemed surprised at the answer, but quickly shrugged it off and started searching through her desk drawer until she brought out her checkbook.

"If you'll give me a total for your fees and expenses, I would be more than happy to write you a check."

Blackthorne bowed deeply and rose with an expression of serene sincerity.

"I do not require any fee for my services, Miss Kirkpatrick. As I said, I charge according to how much time I spend and the degree of difficulty.

"In your case I have spent little time, and I must say, I have thoroughly enjoyed every minute of it. Truly it is I who should pay for the experience."

Again the beautiful Molly Kirkpatrick seemed totally flabbergasted by Blackthorne's words. It was clear she couldn't begin to figure him out and was perplexed and amused by his actions.

"I must insist that you allow me to pay you something, Mr Blackthorne. It would be unfair of me to let you spend so much time and effort, as well as your own money, to find my brother without reimbursing you in some way."

"Please, Miss Kirkpatrick, I will not argue. Besides, we haven't solved all of the details of the case, and I'm not sure we've seen the end of it."

"What do you mean?" she asked, again taken aback by the direction of the conversation.

"We still haven't answered the question of who kidnapped Mr Kirkpatrick or why."

"But I thought he was shanghaied."

"He was."

"But don't dogs get shanghaied all the time? I mean, I read about it in the papers."

"That's true," answered Blackthorne, "but it's usually drunken *sailors* that get snatched, not accountants. It's not very efficient to grab someone who knows nothing about handling the sails on a ship."

"Couldn't they have made a mistake? Maybe they were just kidnapping anybody they could find."

"I hope you are right, Miss Kirkpatrick. Nevertheless, please inform me of any suspicious activity of any kind in the next few weeks. I would like to come back and speak with your brother sometime tomorrow if I might."

"Certainly, but you're making me nervous. If whoever kidnapped him was specifically out to get Patrick, what makes you think they won't just come back again?"

"They won't come to the house, that is certain. They waited till he was on the street the first time, and now that we've got him back, they'll be extra careful. Only when we are sure of the reason behind the criminal's actions can we be sure that your brother is out of danger.

"Please don't worry about anything happening before we tie up all the loose ends. I give you my word that you are safe and secure for the time being.

"I can also give you my most confident assurance that we will soon arrive at a satisfactory conclusion to all of this and you will be able to sleep soundly once again without fear of anything further upsetting the tranquility of your home."

Molly Kirkpatrick appeared to accept him at his word and visibly relaxed. "Very well," she agreed. "I will not worry about a thing until you tell me differently."

She leaned over and kissed Blackthorne on the cheek, and before I could react, gave me a fond peck on my whiskers as well. "I would love for you to come by tomorrow for lunch and refreshments, and I will not take no for an answer. You may ask Patrick all the questions you like over your meal." She raised an eyebrow and turned her stunning features in my direction.

"That goes for you as well, Dr Smithfield. I don't know exactly how you two managed to get Patrick off that ship and out of the paws of those horrible criminals, but I plan to hear all about it."

I'm sure I was blushing, and although I tried to think of a wry comment with just the right amount of devil-may-care attitude, a touch of dashing wit, and a sprinkle of magnetic charm, I was unable to do anything but nod my head.

Thankfully, she once more turned her attention towards Blackthorne. "What time do you eat lunch, Mr Blackthorne?"

"Three o'clock," he finally answered, his lip curling almost imperceptibly with amusement.

"Very well," she nodded with finality. "I will see both of you right here at three P.M. sharp."

I tipped my hat, and Blackthorne buttoned his jacket. Miss Kirkpatrick opened the door and without a word we stepped into the hallway.

"One more thing, gentlemen."

We both stopped and waited for her to finish.

"You had better be hungry when you arrive or you will be thought to have little in the way of manners."

"I think I can speak for both of us," answered Blackthorne, "when I say that you will not be disappointed."

"See you at three."

Blackthorne bowed deeply. "Good night, madam."

17

DO YOU REALLY THINK someone specifically wanted to kidnap Kirkpatrick? Or were you just saying that to get Miss Molly to invite us back again?"

Blackthorne looked sideways at me as if I had just insulted his honour. "I would never even consider the possibility of ever lying to a sincere and beautiful creature like Miss Kirkpatrick merely to prolong her attentions. In fact I find it hard to believe that the idea even occurred to you at all."

"Very well, Blackthorne," I replied. "No need to

get upset about it. I just had no warning that you were thinking these thoughts. You keep so much to yourself that you continually take me by surprise."

"Sorry, old boy, it hadn't occurred to me until after we'd snagged Kirkpatrick that some of the pieces didn't fit together."

We had just turned the corner onto Market Street and were walking back to the apartment through a thick swirl of cool, moist fog. Blackthorne

had suggested making our way on foot rather than taking a cab and I agreed.

It was early and I was still invigorated from our evening's adventure. A brisk walk would clear my head and hopefully calm my fleeting thoughts.

It was apparent that Blackthorne, too, was excited by the events of the day, and he chattered almost non-stop the entire way home.

"Consider this," he said, clasping his paws together, the tails of his green tweed jacket bouncing with his quick, purposeful stride. "Most victims who are shanghaied are knocked on the head late at night when few individuals are on the street. Mr Kirkpatrick disappeared shortly after ten, when there is still a fair amount of foot traffic on the streets.

"Consider this as well, that most shanghai victims are taken after a night of drinking in well-known hangouts for sailors, usually near the wharfs, always in bad neighbourhoods. Kirkpatrick, on the other paw, was in a tavern that caters to accountants and lawyers, not sea dogs. He wasn't drunk either. The bartender said he had coffee and some dinner before he left, nothing alcoholic."

I rolled the points Blackthorne made over and over in my head and came to the same conclusion. Kirkpatrick had obviously been kidnapped for some other reason than to serve as a slave sailor onboard a ship that needed some extra crew members and didn't care how it got them.

"There are other characteristics about the case that don't fit our simple explanation," said Blackthorne. "Usually, when a ship takes delivery of shanghaied sailors, it pays for several at a time. The cost is usually cheaper by the pound, and if one or two are thrown overboard because they are unco-operative or unskilled or both, the ship's captain still has enough left over to maintain a full crew.

"In Kirkpatrick's case, there were no other shanghaied sailors on the ship with him. He wasn't a member of a group of kidnap victims, he was all alone, as if he was the *only* one they wanted."

"But if that's the case," I asked, "then why? What is it about Mr Kirkpatrick that would make some-one want to kidnap him and lock him away on a ship bound for the Orient?"

"That's the key," agreed Blackthorne. "If we knew

that, then all of the other locked doorways would be open to us as well."

"What other doorways?" I asked, wondering what he was getting at.

"In time, Smithfield, in time. For now, however, we need to get over to the Lucky Dog Casino."

"But I thought we were on our way home."

"Of course not, man!" exclaimed Blackthorne, waving down a cab. "I don't turn down dinner invitations from beautiful women so I can go home and spend the evening with you!"

"I did think it was rather odd," I commented. "Whatever, may I ask, are we going to do once we arrive at this particular gambling establishment?"

"We have an appointment, my dear fellow." Blackthorne was once again beaming with that self-satisfied grin, the one that made me nervous every time I saw it.

A chill travelled up my spine as I realised what I thought was going to be a pleasant, early evening in bed with a book was turning out to be only the beginning of an adventure that might lead anywhere or nowhere, but was sure to keep me up well into the late hours, and would take me to places I wasn't sure I wanted to go.

I hesitated to say it, but it was becoming obvious that Blackthorne wasn't going to volunteer the information unless I pried it out of him.

"Who exactly, dare I ask, are we going to see at the notorious Lucky Dog?"

"I'm surprised you haven't guessed," replied Blackthorne. "His name seems to come up everywhere we go."

I sorted through the names and faces we'd seen in the last few days and the cold chill became a few degrees cooler as one name floated to the surface of my thoughts.

"Not Big Bill Powell?" I asked, hoping I was wrong.

"You see," replied Blackthorne, straightening his bow tie, "you knew the answer all along."

18

THE LUCKY DOG CASINO was loud, smoky, and crowded. We made our way to a table near the corner and sat down. After taking in the scene, we ordered drinks. Blackthorne had the usual espresso with cream, and I had a steamed milk with double sugar.

There was a band playing on a stage at one end, and at the other was the longest bar I think I had ever seen. It must have sat a hundred dogs on its red leather and brass stools. The bar top was made of bird's-eye maple, varnished and polished to a deep glow.

Around the room were several dozen tables with groups of dogs and even some cats gathered against them, betting on the action, cheering if they won, complaining if they didn't.

At most of the tables, the participants were playing poker, or various forms of it. At some they threw dice. At others, they played dominoes or backgammon.

One table was filled with gamblers playing blackjack. At another, they were scattered around a large roulette wheel.

Every number shown on the roulette wheel was also painted onto the surface of the table. Dogs would place their bets by stacking chips on whatever number they hoped would win. More often than not, they never got their chips back.

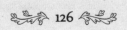

"Once again, you could have warned me," I said to Blackthorne after we received our drinks.

"Oh come on, Smithfield," he replied. "You probably wouldn't have come and then I'd have to sit here by myself."

"But what if Big Bill decides we're too much trouble and kills us or something?"

"Where?" asked Blackthorne. "Here?"

"Sure, here! He just has some of his boys knock us on the head and take us in the back to finish us off."

"Really, Smithfield, you know I wouldn't put you in any danger."

"How can you be so sure?" I was beginning to resent Blackthorne's constant assumption that I wanted to be included in his shady dealings.

"Here he comes now," said Blackthorne.

At first, I wasn't sure what he had said, but I slowly came to the realisation that Big Bill Powell was walking up behind me.

Blackthorne stood on his chair, as he was known to do because of his rather short stature, and extended a paw in greeting. Big Bill Powell seemed to block out the light.

"I'm Bill Powell," said the huge dog.

"Samuel Blackthorne," said Blackthorne. "This is my colleague, Dr Edward Smithfield."

"Pleased to meet you." The huge dog's paw completely covered my own, but he was careful to shake gently enough not to dislocate my elbow.

Until now I had not known what kind of dog Big Bill Powell was, and I had not thought to ask. I suppose I should have known he would be something pretty large, but I wasn't expecting him to be an Irish wolfhound.

He must have weighed more than 160 pounds. His hair was bright red and stuck out in clumps. He was dressed in a black tuxedo. He sat down and turned his attention once more to Blackthorne. "What can I do for you?"

"I wanted to ask you about Patrick Kirkpatrick," said Blackthorne.

"What about him?"

"It seems he was kidnapped last night by two of your boys."

"*My* boys?" asked Bill, seemingly surprised. "Which ones?"

"We don't have any names," said Blackthorne. "Our sources just said they worked for you."

"I'll see what I can find out, but I'll tell you right now, I didn't order anyone kidnapped, especially not him."

"Why not him?" asked Blackthorne.

"Because we're business partners, that's why."

"What kind of business, if I might ask?"

"You may not," answered Bill. "What do you want from me besides accusing me of kidnapping somebody?"

"I wasn't accusing you," said Blackthorne, shaking his head. "I was just telling you that's what we heard."

"Well, you can tell your sources that Bill Powell has never shanghaied anyone. I'm strictly in the gaming industry."

"You mean gambling, don't you?" I said.

"Whatever," answered Bill in an aggravated tone.

"If we thought you did it," said Blackthorne, "we wouldn't be here."

"Then why exactly *are* you here?"

"Details, Mr Powell. I need to fill out the picture

and you might have the missing pieces."

"Why should I tell you anything?"

"Because it's in your best interest, that's why." Blackthorne seemed impatient. "Look, if you didn't know he was missing, you wouldn't have met with me tonight. You obviously want to find him yourself and you thought you might be able to get some information out of me."

Big Bill's eyes were unreadable.

Blackthorne continued. "He was working on something you were interested in, and when he disappeared, you were afraid he had made a better deal with someone else."

"You said this meeting would be in my best interest. So where is he?" asked Big Bill.

"He's at home with his sister," answered Blackthorne. "He's a little tired, but he should be fine within a day or two."

I couldn't believe he had just informed this hoodlum where Mr Kirkpatrick was, but it was too late now, so I decided to wait and see where the conversation led.

"He was building some sort of counting

machine, wasn't he?" asked Blackthorne.

"How should I know?" answered the wolfhound. "Why don't you ask him?"

"Listen, Mr Powell, if you're going to continue to be uncooperative, I won't waste my time trying to help your situation. It is, however, obvious that someone's out to get your Mr Kirkpatrick and his counting machine and you don't have a clue who it is."

"And I suppose you do?"

"I do indeed," replied Blackthorne.

"Then why don't you tell me?"

"Because I have a few questions of my own, first." Big Bill's eyes narrowed beneath furry red brows. "If you're lying, there's nowhere in this town where I can't find you."

"That's a matter of opinion," said Blackthorne. "Nevertheless, I'm not lying. You can choose not to believe me, or you can answer my questions and maybe we'll get whoever is responsible before they get Kirkpatrick."

"Okay, little buddy," said Big Bill. "You don't have to get all huffy about it."

Blackthorne's expression went cold. "I'm not your little buddy."

"Sorry," apologised the wolfhound. "It's just that I can't talk about business until I've had a chance to check out your story. If it was my guys who snatched the kid, I need to know who. I need to talk to Kirkpatrick and find out what happened. After all, I've never met you before and you have to admit, your story sounds pretty far-fetched.

"I'll tell you what," said the wolfhound. "I'll meet you for dinner tomorrow night, and if everything's on the up and up, I'll buy you the best meal in town. Sound fair?"

Blackthorne thought for a moment and then smiled, showing his tiny, pearl white teeth.

"What do you consider the best meal in town?"

"The North Beach Fish House," answered Big Bill without hesitation.

"I will say one thing for you," observed Blackthorne. "You have excellent taste in restaurants."

"When you eat as much as I do," said Big Bill, "it's a necessity."

19

WE ARRIVED AT MOLLY and Patrick Kirkpatrick's home at 3:00 P.M. on the dot. Molly answered the door and invited us in. She took our jackets and showed us to the kitchen table, where Patrick was sitting up and looking considerably more alert than he had been when we last saw him.

Patrick stood when we walked in. "I cannot possibly express my appreciation and gratitude for what both of you have done."

"It was nothing," replied Blackthorne.

"Quite exciting, actually," I added.

Patrick Kirkpatrick shook both of our paws, and we seated ourselves around the well-worn wooden table.

Lunch was still on the stove, and Molly served us each a glass of fresh lemonade while she continued to monitor the various pans, occasionally lifting the lids and giving the contents a stir or a poke. It smelled delicious, and as I didn't usually wait until this late in the afternoon to eat lunch, my mouth was watering and my stomach began to make rumbling noises.

I made a quick visual assessment of Mr Kirkpatrick's condition. "How are you feeling?"

"Pretty good," he answered. "I'm bruised up a bit, but I don't feel dizzy and sick like I did last night."

"Any loss of memory? Headache?"

"A little headache, but that's almost gone. Molly's been pouring hot green tea down my throat all morning and I think that's helping."

"What's the last thing you remember?" asked Blackthorne.

"I was walking down Mission near Beale and a

fellow bumped into me. Nothing after that, until you rescued me."

At this point Molly brought us each a small spinach salad with mushrooms, bacon, and Swiss cheese, over which she drizzled a dressing made from honey, mustard, and the drippings from the bacon.

We enjoyed our salads for a few minutes and Blackthorne made small yummy noises that I don't think he was even aware of. He wiped his goatee carefully with his napkin and sighed with the satisfaction of someone who genuinely appreciates a truly fine meal.

"I must say, Miss Kirkpatrick, it isn't often that Smithfield and myself get treated to such care and attention, and it is truly rare that it is administered by someone of your exceptional qualities."

Miss Kirkpatrick smiled and, apparently somewhat embarrassed by Blackthorne's compliment, bent her head and gathered another forkful of salad. "You are too kind, Mr Blackthorne, but the pleasure is all mine."

I had never witnessed this kind of response from Blackthorne towards a member of the gentler sex.

Usually he was polite, but he could also be prone to impatience and even arrogance. His gracious compliments and boyish manner both surprised and amused me, and I watched this new side of his personality with interest.

The main course was breast of quail with baby carrots and garlic mashed potatoes. The plates were beautifully arranged with a sprig of rosemary and a lovely lime green sauce.

After a period of small talk and another round of complimentary comments on the magnificent food, Blackthorne once more returned to the business at hand.

"May I ask about the counting machine?"

Kirkpatrick, in the process of putting a forkful of mashed potatoes in his mouth, stopped and blinked in astonishment.

"How did you know about that?"

"It was the only explanation," replied Blackthorne. "We examined your room for clues to your whereabouts, and I noticed your interest in number theory as well as mechanical devices. That, combined with your profession as an accountant and your association with Big Bill Powell, led me to the obvious conclusion."

"Good heavens!" exclaimed Mr Kirkpatrick. "No wonder Molly came to you for help. Your intellect is astounding!"

Blackthorne shrugged. "Thank you for the compliment, but it's really a fairly simple matter of acute observation and application of deductive reasoning."

"Big Bill Powell?" asked Molly. "What kind of association are you talking about? I thought he was the one who shanghaied poor Patrick?"

"Not exactly," answered Blackthorne. "Apparently, someone else managed to hire away two of Big Bill's boys to crack old Patrick on the head and deliver him to the *Cuthbert.*"

"It's my fault," said Patrick to Molly. "I should have told you, but I thought you'd be upset with me for dealing with a dog of Big Bill's unsavory reputation."

"What are you talking about?" asked Molly, becoming even more perplexed.

"I couldn't help it," explained Patrick. "I have been working on a machine that can count and add numbers over and over again with absolute and perfect accuracy."

Molly remained quiet, and after taking a sip of lemonade, Patrick continued.

"The potential for such a device is almost unlimited. It could be used for accounting, obviously. Inventories, schedules, the census, bookkeeping of all kinds could be done more quickly and easily without the time-consuming need for calculating and rechecking each and every figure.

"If everyone had a machine of this sort, ever larger numbers could be simply and efficiently added, subtracted, multiplied, and even divided, by individuals of limited mathematical ability."

As he talked Patrick Kirkpatrick became more

animated and enthusiastic. It was obvious that he was consumed with passion about the device and its potential.

"No longer would mathematics be the sole realm of the highly educated. Instead of being some mysterious, magical science out of reach of regular dogs, maths would become an everyday tool to be used by common individuals to help them run their businesses more effectively, predict the movement of the stars, engineer better bridges and buildings; there's no limit to what we could do."

"But what does that have to do with Big Bill Powell?" asked Molly. "I thought we were through with him years ago."

Patrick's eyes moved from Blackthorne to me and back as Blackthorne polished off the last of the tasty morsels on his plate.

"What Molly is referring to is our association with the Bayview Racecourse. After our parents died, we found ourselves penniless and with no prospects to make a living. I had two years of college under my belt, but without money I would not be able to graduate. We were facing a life of hard labour, long hours, and starvation wages unless we could find a way out."

Kirkpatrick took a long swallow of lemonade.

"It was Molly who came up with the idea. She was the fastest runner in our neighbourhood. She had never lost a race, against anyone. We decided to go down to the track and see what kind of a living one could make as a racer. That's when we met Big Bill Powell.

"Anyway, Big Bill could spot a gifted racer the first time he saw Molly run, and he hired her on the spot. I wasn't nearly as fast, but he gave me a job filling out the pack in races where they needed a warm body. But Molly was the star."

At this point Molly stood up and started to collect the plates from the table. Her shyness and modesty became apparent as her brother heaped on the admiration and she busied herself with rinsing the dishes.

"We made enough money, or I should say Molly made enough money, for me to finish school, and we were saving for *her* education when an injury forced her to quit racing.

"Well, without Molly, they weren't very interested in keeping me on. So we decided the smartest thing to do was for me to get my degree and start working in a profession as soon as possible. Once I got a job, then I would use part of my earnings to put Molly through school as well."

"A noble plan," I commented.

"Thanks," said Patrick. "So that's what we've been doing for the past seven years. Molly graduated in the top of her class and is currently finishing up a medical degree from the University of San Francisco."

"Excellent," I exclaimed, feeling ashamed of myself for never asking Miss Kirkpatrick about the details of her life. She had said she was a student and had not gone any further. "That is precisely the institution where I obtained my own degree nearly two decades ago!"

"I know," replied Miss Kirkpatrick. "I saw your diploma on the wall of your lodgings."

"You two classmates can catch up later," said Blackthorne. "Meanwhile Mr Kirkpatrick hasn't finished his story."

"Very well," continued Patrick. "I came up with

the idea of a counting machine about a year ago and have recently been consulting with machinists to manufacture a working model.

"The problem, once again, became a lack of money. It costs an enormous amount to assemble the gears and levers and springs necessary to produce even the simplest design. In order to protect my ideas, I had to hire a lawyer to file for patents and to draw up contracts with the various specialists I required.

"I had to find a source of financing, and when I went to banks they dismissed me as a crackpot."

"Bankers aren't known for their creativity," observed Blackthorne, "or their intelligence."

"Isn't that the truth," agreed Patrick. "Anyway, I was turned down over and over again and I had about given up, when I had the idea to go to Big Bill Powell. I started thinking about the uses a counting machine could be put to at the racetrack and it seemed like a natural fit.

"Not only would the ability to add large numbers quickly be helpful in figuring the gambling odds for each race, it would help eliminate dishonesty among the track employees. It's much more difficult to skim money if a machine is keeping track of it.

"Also, by using telegraph machines, bets could be placed at locations all over town and then be electronically wired to the track where a counting machine could tally the figures.

"The payroll costs of the track would be cut down because it wouldn't take as many dogs to add the figures and check them and calculate the odds, and all the other mathematical operations that must be performed constantly to keep the track running smoothly.

"With faster arithmetic the time between races could also be cut down and more races could be run each day. All in all, profits would skyrocket."

"So Big Bill agreed to finance your invention if you would put it to use for him first," said Blackthorne.

"That's right," confirmed Kirkpatrick. "That's why it didn't make sense when Molly told me it was Big Bill's boys that knocked me on the head."

"That threw me for a loop, too," said Blackthorne. "Big Bill's a shady character, but he has a nose for profits, and there's certainly no profit in getting rid of you before you've had a chance to finish your machine."

"Did you notice anything missing amongst your belongings?" asked Blackthorne. "Your sister told us of your diagrams, but your desk was virtually empty."

"I haven't really had a chance to check," answered Patrick. "But most of my designs are already at the machinists' or the lawyers' offices."

"Do you ever associate with any cats?"

The greyhound blinked twice and shook his head. "I don't think so. I mean I don't have anything against them. I just don't really know any."

"So you've never had a cat over to visit, or anything like that?"

He turned to Molly. "You?"

"No," answered the graceful greyhound. "Why do you ask?"

"It's probably nothing," answered Blackthorne. "I'm just trying to cover any possibilities. Can you think of anyone who would want to steal your counting machine or anyone who might have a grudge against you?"

"Not really," said Patrick. "I mean I'm sure there are dogs who might want my plans, but I wouldn't know who that might be. Most everyone thinks I'm crazy when I talk about it.

"As far as someone wanting to shanghai me because they have a grudge, I can't think of anyone. I keep to myself mostly, and I try to be nice to everyone."

"Well, then." Blackthorne pushed himself back from the table and folded his napkin. "I think I may know who's behind all this, but I've got a few more things to check on before I disclose my theories."

"If it's not Big Bill Powell, then who could it possibly be?" asked Molly.

"I'd rather wait before I go spouting off," said Blackthorne. "After all, your brother's not the only one who has been called crazy for his ideas."

"Shouldn't you go to the police?"

Blackthorne clasped his paws over his stomach, now visibly full after the delectable meal he had just eaten. "You've seen for yourself how much assistance the police have been up till now.

"No, I think it's better to wait until we're sure what we're dealing with before asking for their assistance. I'm sure they mean well, but in this town it's sometimes better to keep things to yourself as long as possible. You never know who's listening."

"Can I interest you in some coffee or cappuccino?" asked Molly.

"You are too kind," replied Blackthorne, "but I'm afraid Dr Smithfield and I have to check on a few things before this evening, and we must hurry if we are to get it all done in time for our dinner engagement." He patted his stomach and it made a sound like a ripe watermelon. "After that most excellent meal, I'm not sure if we'll be able to eat much more than a small appetizer."

"Whom are you having dinner with? If I may ask," said Mr Kirkpatrick.

"Your friend Big Bill Powell," answered Blackthorne. "I think he might be able to be of assistance in this matter. After all, he doesn't want you disappearing again either."

Blackthorne wiped his whiskers and gave Molly Kirkpatrick a wink. "Besides, I never turn down an invitation to a good meal."

20

A USUAL BLACKTHORNE didn't tell me where we were headed, and despite my insistent questioning, he chose to remain silent on the matter.

The ocean breeze was just beginning to turn cool, and he sniffed at the wind as the taxi drove through the cobblestone streets.

He signalled for the cabby to stop at a storefront bakery, and he dashed inside while I stayed in the taxi and wondered where our adventures would take us next.

Although I am a somewhat quiet individual who prefers a cup of hot cocoa and a good book to a night on the town, I found myself filled with an excitement and anticipation I had thought was gone forever from my tired and rather dull existence.

As I sat watching the fog beginning to roll down the hills and over the buildings towards the bay, I realised that despite Blackthorne's eccentric personality and frequently odd behaviour, my association with him had restored a glimmer of something the French call *joie de vivre*, the joy of life, in me.

Since my injury I had let my thoughts turn inwards, and I became less and less concerned with the world outside myself. Blackthorne had shown me that to place oneself in the middle of events, to pursue subjects and experiences that may be difficult or inconvenient, can bring one a sense of involvement and participation in the business of life.

Upon reflection I realised my leg hurt less than it usually did. In fact I had not been aware of any pain at all for long periods of time over the last few days. Whatever effect Samuel Blackthorne had on me seemed to agree with my general health and attitude towards life.

What I didn't know at the time was that things were about to change for the worse, and if I wasn't exceptionally careful, both my health and my life itself were about to be put at dire risk.

It was nearly 5:00 P.M. when we arrived at San Francisco City Hall. We descended the stairs and proceeded down a series of corridors before entering a wooden door with a pebbled glass window labelled RECORDS DEPARTMENT.

Sitting at a desk inside was a rather old, stooped-over Maltese lady, who didn't seem to notice us as we stood waiting. Not knowing our purpose here, I left it to Blackthorne to decide what to do. He remained standing for nearly a minute before she lifted her head and peered over her glasses.

Blackthorne raised an eyebrow and a smile slowly began to spread across the Maltese matron's face.

He held the box he had purchased from the bakery out to her, and she took it with obvious anticipation.

"You are such a sweet young man," she said, as

she opened the lid to see what it held.

"It is the least I can do for someone of your beauty and wisdom," said Blackthorne.

She tilted her head and pulled at her matted and stringy white hair. As her smile grew I could see that she was missing at least half of her teeth, and by the colour and general condition of the ones remaining, she was on the verge of losing the other half.

Blackthorne introduced me, and as I reached out to shake paws, she used the other paw to stuff a large portion of a cream puff into her mouth.

"Mrs Cardiccio, may I present my friend Dr Edward Smithfield, who is assisting me in some of my researches."

"Pleased to meet you," I said. Her reply was muffled by the pastry she was attempting to chew into pieces small enough to swallow.

Once she had downed the remains of the mouthful, she spoke again. "You know we close in thirty minutes."

Blackthorne nodded apologetically. "With your talents, my dear, I think that should be plenty of time."

"If I were fifty years younger," she waggled her paw at him, "you'd be in big trouble."

"If you were fifty years younger, Mrs Cardiccio," said Blackthorne, "I have no doubt I would never get anything at all accomplished."

She broke into a raucous laugh, and despite her lack of teeth, I could imagine, for a moment, how beautiful she might have been when she was young.

She polished off the last of the cream puff and her face once more became serious.

"Okay, Mr B., what are we looking for?"

Blackthorne produced a small piece of paper on which was written a list of local gambling establishments.

"I need to know which ones have changed

ownership in the last year or so and who bought them."

She looked the list up and down, and then with a groan, stood up and pushed the chair out from behind her. "This way, gentlemen," she motioned as she waddled back towards row after row of filing cabinets and shelf after shelf of dusty, leather-bound books.

We followed her until she came to a tall green filing cabinet where she used a step stool to climb up and open one of the drawers. She brought several files over to a nearby table and lit a gas lamp to illuminate its surface. Blackthorne sat down and began to read through the files' contents.

Mrs Cardiccio continued to bring files as Blackthorne copied down names and addresses. When she was finished, he then gave her this new list from which she would then locate even more files, and so on and so on.

As I watched him work, I was again impressed by his ability to absorb and process information. He consumed each file the way Mrs Cardiccio had consumed the cream puff, hungrily, in large chunks, until there was nothing left.

When he had finished, he offered to help put away the stack of files, but Mrs Cardiccio would have none of it.

"I'll put these things away tomorrow morning," she scolded, as if his volunteering to help were an insult to her position. "Meanwhile you boys need to get out of here so I can close up shop."

"Once again your expertise and efficiency have proved indispensable to our investigations," said Blackthorne with a dramatic bow.

"Get outta here," scolded Mrs Cardiccio, "before I grab you and give you a kiss right in front of your friend here."

Blackthorne smiled and turned to leave. I tipped my hat and followed him out.

We were nearly into the hallway when she called out to us.

"Have I ever told you how much I adore lemon meringue pie?"

"You certainly have, my dear," replied Blackthorne, before closing the door behind him. "Many times."

21

THE NORTH BEACH FISH HOUSE was one of the oldest restaurants in the city. It had started out as a small eatery, serving the freshest of whatever the fishermen had caught that day, and as the number of satisfied customers grew, the owners added on one room after another.

Currently, it was a maze of dining rooms full of mismatched tables and chairs and a motley crew of waiters, waitresses, bartenders, and busboys who were boisterous, a little rough around the edges, and extremely good at their jobs.

The menu was written on a blackboard near the entrance, and one never knew of what the meals would consist until the chief cook had selected the day's catch from the nets of the returning ships.

Big Bill was already there when we entered, and he was just finishing a large platter of oysters, washed down with a huge mug of dark, foamy beer.

"Sit down, sit down, boys! I was beginning to think you weren't going to show!"

"I apologise for our tardiness," said Blackthorne. "We've just come from City Hall and our research took longer than expected."

"No problem," answered Bill with a hearty laugh. "Let's get you boys something to drink and then we can get down to eatin' some fish." He motioned to a waitress and she came over to take our orders.

Bill waited until we had a few sips, coffee for Blackthorne and warm milk for me, before he questioned us about City Hall.

"What did you find out?" he asked, leaning forward with anticipation.

"It seems that someone is buying up all the casinos in town," said Blackthorne. "Virtually everyone who's anyone has sold out in the past nine months."

"Sold out?" asked Bill sarcastically. "Been run out is more accurate, I think."

"How so?" asked Blackthorne.

"Nobody ever sells a casino," said Bill, stuffing the last oyster into his huge mouth. "The kind of dogs that go into this business don't usually retire, and they certainly don't give up easily. But my competitors are disappearing one by one."

He held out a huge, red furry paw and started folding back individual claws as he counted them off. "Rabbit Wilson went on a fishing trip and never came back. Henry Styles drowned in his bathtub. Frank Nelson fell down a flight of stairs and broke his neck." He took a swallow of beer that drained the mug. "Have you ever heard of a dog falling down a flight of stairs?"

"Who do you think is behind it?" asked Blackthorne.

"I don't know," said Bill, shaking his big head. "I put the word out that I wanted to talk to the two boys that kidnapped your friend. So far, they haven't turned up."

"They probably won't," observed Blackthorne. "By now they're on their way to China themselves, or on the bottom of the sea."

"Did you get any names from City Hall?" asked Bill.

"Not much," answered Blackthorne. "Corporations mostly, owned by other corporations; holding companies, silent partners, family trusts, every one of them trailing off into nothingness."

Blackthorne sipped his coffee and his eyes became slits as he showed his frustration. "Out of twenty-two gambling establishments that have changed ownership, none of them, not one, was sold to a dog with a simple name and address. There is no doubt that whoever is buying everything up does not want anyone finding out his or her identity."

Blackthorne looked at Big Bill. "Have you been threatened or intimidated in any way?"

Big Bill laughed with a deep, throaty sound that

momentarily drowned out the dull roar of the other tables around them.

"Nobody intimidates me," he said with a gleam in his eye that gave me the chills. "There have been a few . . . instances, though. One of my places was burned last week, and the cops have been coming down pretty hard on me lately."

He appeared to remember something. "Now that I think about it, a guy did try to kill me about a month ago. Would you believe he tried to drop a cement block on my head?"

"Did you catch him?" asked Blackthorne.

"Not exactly," answered Bill. "Unfortunately for him."

"Well who was it? Did you find out why he did it? Who hired him?"

Bill got a look of disappointment on his face. "There were two of them actually. One of them was a cat. He got away."

"What about the other?" I asked, my curiosity getting the better of me.

"He didn't make it," answered Bill with a grimace.

"Then where is he?" I prodded.

"He tried to follow the cat across a ledge and fell. When we got to him he was already dead." Bill shook his head at the memory. "Cats. They're like ghosts or something. Always sneaking around on the rooftops and such. They're creepy, I tell you, downright creepy."

"Was he, by any chance, orange?" asked Blackthorne.

Big Bill's eyes widened. "Sure was. How did you know?"

"I think our feline friend was in Mr Kirkpatrick's apartment the night he disappeared."

"You think a cat's behind this?" asked Bill, surprised.

"I'm not sure," answered Blackthorne. "But there is no doubt there is more here than meets the eye, and that cat, whoever he is, won't give up until you sell the casino."

"That may be," said Bill. "But even if I wanted to, no one has approached me with an offer."

"That's because they know you wouldn't take a deal anyway, no matter what the price."

"Then there's only one thing left to do," said Bill.

"That's right," agreed Blackthorne. "The only way they're going to get your businesses is to get rid of you."

"Get rid of you how?" I asked.

"Kill me, of course," answered Bill, a large smile on his face. "More oysters?"

22

THE FOLLOWING DAYS proved to be dreary and depressing. It rained constantly and the sky was dark and gloomy. Blackthorne stayed in his room most of the day, only coming out to use the bathroom or make himself a small snack, which he then took back to his room to eat in silence.

Several times I tried to start a conversation, but he would always mumble something and walk away as if he were in a mental haze as thick as the fog that rolled in over the city every evening.

Once, in the afternoon, I came home to find

him still in his housecoat, carefully watering and trimming the tiny bonsai tree. I thought he must be coming out of his funk and would soon return to the old Blackthorne, pacing the floor, expounding on a variety of diverse subjects, and dashing off to a hundred destinations at all times of the night and day.

But it was not to be. Without a word, he set the small watering can back in its place on the shelf above the stove, replaced the stainless steel trimmers in the drawer, and returned to his room, where he stayed until the next day.

One evening I awoke to a *thunking* sound coming from the living room. When I ventured out to see what it was, I found Blackthorne carefully aiming and shooting a small, precision-made crossbow.

Lined up in front of a thick wooden plank was a series of lighted candles, which were extinguished, one by one, as their wicks were severed by the razor-sharp tip of the steel darts.

The next night, around 1:00 A.M. when I went to the bathroom, I noticed him sitting by the glowing embers of the fireplace, reading through a packet of postcards that had been tied with a pink, silk ribbon.

They were written in a female's delicate, flowing script, and the stamps were French. I couldn't see the postmark, but by the look of the paper, they were quite old.

I walked past and he looked up for a minute without changing his expression.

I went back to bed and worried that he might not come out of his dark mood ever again.

The next morning I made up my mind to confront him with his behaviour and take some sort of action if it became necessary. I brushed my teeth and trimmed my beard while rehearsing what I was going to say. The fact was, Blackthorne had been in a slump for too long and someone needed to do something. I wasn't sure exactly what course of action I was going to pursue, but I figured I had to start somewhere and that was with Blackthorne himself.

He was sitting in the living room, staring out the window, when I poured myself a cup of tea and joined him.

"How are you this morning, Smithfield?" he beamed.

"I was about to ask you the same question," I replied. "You've been something of a bear these last few days."

"I'm sorry, Smithfield. I know I haven't been very polite lately, and I hope I haven't spoiled your opinion of me. It's just that I was having trouble figuring this one out and it sometimes gets the better of me."

"You seem to be much improved today," I said, noticing how the colour had returned to his face and his eyes didn't look as tired as they had the night before. Apparently he had managed to get some sleep.

"I feel considerably better," confirmed Blackthorne. "You see, I have narrowed it down to only a few individuals who would have the resources and motivation to try to control every major gambling establishment in the entire city."

"Whom did you come up with?"

"That's the problem," he answered. "I don't know which one is the culprit. I need something to happen."

"What do you mean?" I asked.

"I need for whoever is behind all this to come out in the open. I need him to make a move."

"What about the cat?"

"I don't think we'll see him," said Blackthorne. "He's going to want to lay low for a while, and now that we know what he looks like, he can't sneak around without someone noticing. I think we'll see something from a different direction."

I still wasn't quite sure I understood where he was heading. "You're not making yourself clear," I said. "What kind of thing are you expecting to see?"

"Oh, you know." Blackthorne's attention was drawn by something outside the window on the street. "Maybe an assassin."

I held a reply because I wasn't sure I had heard him correctly.

"You mean you expect someone to try to kill you?"

"You, too, if I'm right," answered Blackthorne with no apparent concern in his voice. "But don't get worried, old boy. I don't think our villain is going to be so crude at this point in time. After all, if he were going to kill us, he would have already done it."

"Well, that's certainly a relief," I commented sarcastically.

"No, I think he'll do something that requires more planning. That's why it has taken so long." Blackthorne stood up and directed his attention onto the street below. "Brilliant! That's it!"

"That's what?" I asked, feeling completely ignorant.

"The solution to our problem, of course!"

"What exactly are you talking about?"

"Don't you see?" Blackthorne's eyes glittered with excitement. "We are about to be arrested."

I looked outside and there was a police wagon parked at the curb. Beside it stood a large rottweiler wearing the familiar uniform of the San Francisco Police Department.

Just then there was a knock at the door.

23

A S WE SAT in our police cell I tried to recall the chain of events that had led up to our current predicament. If I had only decided to go straight to a hotel and bed on the night I arrived, I would never have met Samuel Blackthorne and would never have ended up sleeping on a cold metal cot surrounded by criminals of various degrees of aggressiveness and personal cleanliness.

The prison consisted of four large cells, each holding around a dozen inmates. There were cots attached to the walls like shelves, and I had been lying on my back listening to Blackthorne chatter from the bunk above mine for the last twelve hours.

The police had arrived at the door with a warrant for our arrest that morning. Later in the day we were called before a judge who read us the charges of murder and set our bail at ten thousand dollars each.

Despite my dismay at facing life in prison or worse, Blackthorne seemed not only unconcerned but downright elated at the fact that we were being framed for a crime we didn't commit.

It seems the two dogs who originally kidnapped Patrick Kirkpatrick had ended up floating in the bay and the police had received several "reports" that Blackthorne and I were the culprits. The judge refused to tell us what evidence they had against us and threatened to have me put in chains when I protested our treatment.

Being a generally law-abiding citizen, I had never before seen the inside of a prison cell and I was beginning to become discouraged as the hours passed.

For his part Blackthorne seemed overjoyed. He continued to rattle on about how the fact that we were being falsely arrested narrowed our villain down to only two possible suspects.

"Don't you see, Smithfield? Very few dogs have the influence to actually have someone arrested. Whoever is behind all this has strong connections to city government, which includes the police department and possibly the justice system as well. That means political organisations, campaign contributions, union ties . . . It has to be someone pretty high up in San Francisco society."

"Surely you don't think they stand a chance of convicting us of the murder of those two dogs?" I asked, wishing to be out of this cell and back to my old, uneventful and boring, yet relatively safe, life.

"No, of course not," he answered from the bunk above me. "I'm sure they don't have enough hard evidence to stand up in court. No, they are merely trying to keep us out of the way for a while and ruin our credibility in the process. Certainly no one is going to believe any wild accusations coming from a couple of suspected murderers."

"How long do you think we'll have to endure this indignity?" I was trying to remain calm.

"No more than a month or two, I should imagine."

I felt my heart begin to flutter and I became dizzy with fear and despair.

"That is," continued Blackthorne, "if they don't decide to kill us first."

"But I thought you said they would have already committed that foul act if killing us was in their plans."

"I did, I did," answered Blackthorne. "But that was before we were arrested. Now that we are in prison and charged with a horrendous crime, it would be a simple thing to send in a couple of thugs to strangle us in our sleep. Prisoners are known to be a violent bunch and no one would suspect a thing if we turned up dead one night. We certainly can't defend our reputations if we aren't alive to do it."

"How can you sound so cheerful when we're looking at the possibility of death or prison or both?" I was flabbergasted that he was so delighted by the thought of our imminent deaths.

"Because," he answered, "now that we know our villain is someone with influence in the police department, it should be an easy thing to smoke them out of hiding."

"May I remind you," I gritted my teeth as I became more angry, "that we are locked inside a prison cell!"

"That is an inconvenience," he answered, "but I have no doubt a solution will present itself in time and then we will make our move."

"Our move? Are you kidding? We aren't going to be making any moves if we are in prison!"

"I know you are upset," said Blackthorne in his most reassuring voice, "and I apologise for not anticipating this turn of events sooner. But I'm confident we will eventually extricate ourselves from this state of affairs."

"Your optimism does not exactly fill me with confidence," I replied with a growl.

"Don't worry, my friend. I will not let anything happen to you."

I turned over on my side and tried to get comfortable on the cold metal surface. "I believe you've already broken that promise."

24

I WAS LYING on the bunk, feeling sorry for myself and becoming angrier by the minute, when a loud commotion interrupted my thoughts. Two rather large, brown, ugly pit bulls were thrown into our cell amid some scuffling and snarling by the guards.

The cell door clanged shut, and the new prisoners, almost identical in looks except for the location and severity of their numerous scars, gradually quieted down and found two empty bunks to sit on until it was their turn to see a judge.

Over the course of the night more and more dogs were thrown into the cell in various stages of drunkenness and physical injury. There was no doubt many had been arrested for fighting as they had cuts and bite marks around their faces as well as obvious bruises and sore spots.

Although I wasn't expecting to get any sleep anyway, the clanging doors, shouting guards, growling prisoners, and harsh light from the kerosene lanterns made it all but impossible to relax.

For his part Blackthorne continued to be confident and excited, although he wasn't as talkative as he had been earlier, since I had made it clear I wanted nothing to do with his newest theories or constant plotting.

Towards the early morning hours the cell became overcrowded and the larger, meaner dogs began to bully and push the smaller dogs off the available bunks as in an aggressive game of musical chairs. I was waiting for my turn, and sure enough, it came in the form of a Doberman, whose black, piercing eyes swept the cell until they locked on to me.

I tried not to catch his gaze, but I could feel his

presence as he came closer and stopped at my bunk. His breath smelled stale and rotten, and I could feel myself beginning to tremble as I waited for him to confront me.

"That's my bunk."

I looked up at the angry black eyes.

"I'm sorry, I didn't know this was yours," I answered. "I didn't realise we had assigned sleeping arrangements."

"Listen, you smart-aleck punk," growled the Doberman. "You either move your hindquarters off my bed or I'll chop you up and eat you for dinner."

"There's no need to threaten," came the voice from the top bunk. "Just because you're stupid doesn't mean you can't be polite."

Blackthorne was peering over the edge of the metal bed at the scowling Doberman. He did not seem at all nervous or intimidated by the larger dog, but I could not help but think he was making a valiant attempt to distract the bully rather than a genuine physical challenge.

I don't care what kind of exotic fighting techniques Blackthorne was planning on using: if it came down to violence, I could not help but feel my small companion would be the loser.

Despite my current anger towards Blackthorne for getting us into this situation in the first place, I could not allow him to suffer physical harm on my behalf.

"I would be more than happy to give you my bed, sir!" I declared. "I was beginning to get a stiff back anyway and I need to move around and stretch my muscles."

"Shut up," barked the Doberman. He then turned back towards Blackthorne and his lips began to curl into a snarl. "I mean to tear this little piece of cat poop to shreds."

Blackthorne tensed and I could see him assume a fighting stance. I scanned the cell for anything I might use as a weapon but quickly came to the conclusion that I would have to attack with only my teeth and claws. I took a deep breath and prepared for a painful, certain death.

Then I heard a low, menacing voice come from behind me and to my left.

"Don't even think about it."

The Doberman squinted his black eyes and turned towards the voice.

There stood one of the brown pit bulls with a look of pure evil on his scarred face.

"Who are you?" asked the Doberman.

"I'm just somebody who doesn't like to see wimps like you picking on little dogs who were minding their own business."

The Doberman grinned at the pit bull. "This isn't your fight, friend. Don't be sticking your snout where it doesn't belong or I might have to take care of you when I'm finished with him."

"Save some for me, too," said another voice, as the second of the twin pit bulls stepped forward into the glare of the kerosene light.

"I don't get it," said the Doberman. "What's it to you whether or not I thrash this guy? I got no bone to pick with either of you two."

"You will if you so much as muss up his hair," answered the first pit bull.

I couldn't believe what I was hearing.

Out of nowhere these two hardened street brawlers were intervening on our behalf for no apparent reason other than what appeared to be a noble gesture of fair play and genuine concern.

Blackthorne was still in his fighting stance, and my heart was beating so hard I was sure it was about to burst from my chest.

The Doberman stared at the twins for a few seconds, then levelled his gaze at Blackthorne, who chose that particular moment to arch one eyebrow and wink at the dog, further infuriating him.

Finally, realising that the odds were impossible, the Doberman gave in and retreated to the far corner of the cell.

I closed my mouth, which was still gaping from surprise, and tried to calm myself while Blackthorne grinned from ear to ear and thrust out his paw to shake with the two rescuers.

"Gentlemen," said Blackthorne, "I am indebted to both of you."

"As am I," I sputtered. "I must apologise for starting this whole thing. I probably should have just given him my bunk and none of this would have happened."

"Nonsense," remarked Blackthorne. "Life is too short to allow bullies to rule our behaviour. Besides, I don't think it would have mattered what you did or said. Our friend over there was going to start a fight whether either of us gave him a reason or not."

"I must thank you as well," I said to Blackthorne. "You did not have to come to my defense."

"Of course I did," replied Blackthorne, still smiling. "That's what friends are for."

He turned to the twins. "And speaking of friends, we have certainly made two new ones this evening. I am Samuel Blackthorne and my comrade is Edward Smithfield. Pleased to make your acquaintance."

The pit bulls nodded and the one on the left spoke. "Pleased to meet you. We're Jerry and Mike Cruddles."

"That was a very unselfish thing you just did," I said, shaking their paws in turn. "I did not think there were still dogs around with that kind of honour and integrity."

"Don't get carried away," said the pit bull on the right. "Big Bill asked us to keep an eye on you while you were here."

Just as I thought I was getting used to the constant surprises of the last few days, I was again taken aback by this unexpected revelation.

"You mean you had yourself deliberately arrested for the express purpose of protecting us?"

"It ain't no big deal," said the one on the left. "We usually end up here one or two nights a week anyway."

The other pit bull, Mike, finished the thought. "We like to get drunk and fight."

"Especially fight." Jerry grinned.

"Nevertheless," said Blackthorne, "we are indebted to you and hopefully, one day, you will give us the chance to return the favour."

"Deal," said Jerry. Mike nodded in agreement.

"Why didn't you notify us of your true intentions earlier?" I asked the Cruddles brothers.

"Didn't want to tip anybody off," said Mike.

"Weren't sure who it was going to be," said Jerry.

"Of course," agreed Blackthorne. "The first rule

in the art of war: Don't let your opponent know where the attack is coming from."

The twin brothers gave each other a sideways glance and rolled their eyes. Blackthorne didn't appear to notice, or if he did, he chose not to acknowledge it.

"Bill said to tell you he's working on getting you out," said Jerry.

"He said he just had to make a few arrangements, wouldn't take long," said Mike.

"Well," replied Blackthorne, blinking at the thought of Big Bill intervening on our behalf. "I had no idea we had so many friends watching out for us."

"He couldn't possibly be thinking of bailing us out," I remarked. "Why, together it would total twenty thousand dollars!"

"I think that's exactly what he's doing," said Jerry.

"Takes a while to get up that much cash," said Mike.

"Bill told us you were important," said Jerry.

"He said to make sure nothing bad happened to you guys," said Mike.

At that moment, the door to the cell clanged open and the guard called out the names of Blackthorne and myself.

"Somebody's paid your bail," said the gruff guard as we stepped past him into the brick-and-concrete corridor. He slammed the door behind us and we could hear the metallic chunk of the lock catching hold.

As we were ushered out I looked back at the two brothers. Whether Big Bill had given them orders or not, I couldn't help but feel a sense of gratitude and affection for their having saved us from an almost certainly violent and gruesome fate.

25

OUTSIDE THE PRISON Big Bill was waiting, along with a third pit bull nearly identical to the two we had left inside. He shook our paws and we rode to our apartment for a quick shower and change of clothes.

Several times on the way over, Blackthorne would offer appreciation and gratitude for Big Bill's help with not only the bail money, but also the protection of the Cruddles brothers. Each time, however, Bill would tell him to wait until we had a chance to relax before discussing business.

When we were refreshed and groomed, we travelled to the North Beach Fish House, where Bill relentlessly stuffed us with several courses of the finest seafood on the West Coast.

It was only after we were thoroughly restored both spiritually and nutritionally that Bill lit a cigar and leaned back in his chair. He studied Blackthorne for a minute and gave me a look as if he were sizing us up.

"I did some checking while you two were tied up," said Bill. "I found out who hired my boys away from me. Wouldn't you know it was a cat?"

He said it as if he were disappointed, as if the fact that it was a cat made things somehow more tragic, more humiliating.

"What's his name?" asked Blackthorne. "Whom does he work for?"

"Can't tell you," answered Bill. "Nobody around here's seen him before. But he's a shorthair, light orange, like an apricot. Apparently he's French or something, speaks with an accent, and one more thing" – Bill took another puff on his cigar – "he's only got one ear."

"So you think it was the same cat that was seen running from the scene when you were nearly killed?"

"I didn't get a good enough look to see if it was missing any ears, but if I was a betting dog, and I am, I'd put money on it."

"Speaking of money," I interjected, "I would like to assure you, Mr Powell, that you will get all of your money back when the time comes, and we will reimburse you with interest for your generosity and concern regarding our bail money."

"That's not necessary," said Big Bill. "It's in my best interest to have you guys out and on my team. You two seem to be the only ones that know what's going on. If I lose you, I won't have any help at all."

"We appreciate your help," said Blackthorne, "and all that Smithfield said is the truth, but I would like to make it clear that we're not on anyone's *team*, and just because we have the same enemy, does not mean that we are friends."

"I see your point," laughed Big Bill. "I know you don't approve of my business. I'm not always the most law-abiding dog you'll ever meet, but my games are honest and I don't lie to my friends. Until you give me reason to think differently, I'm going to assume I can trust you. Whether you trust me or not is your own business."

"You have given me no reason not to," said Blackthorne. I nodded in agreement.

After all, Big Bill might be what some called a mobster, but he seemed to have more integrity than the police, and he had certainly got us out of two very bad situations. In spite of myself, I was beginning to enjoy his company.

"You know, they're probably going to try to kill you now," said Big Bill. "Since you've been released."

"That's true," agreed Blackthorne calmly. "I hope they don't use the cement block on the head technique. That sounds messy."

I envisioned the effect of a large concrete block falling onto one's head from a great height. I winced at the thought.

"I don't think you'll have to worry about that

one," said Bill. "It didn't work too well the first time."

"I can't believe what I'm hearing!" I exclaimed, sputtering. "All three of us are going to spend the rest of our lives looking over our shoulder, or above our heads, waiting for someone to try to kill us, and you two are joking about it!"

"Relax," laughed Bill. "Dwight here is going to be your escort until we get this thing cleared up." He nodded at the brown pit bull who was apparently the brother of Jerry and Mike. Dwight was standing near the bar, scanning the crowd and drinking coffee. "There's no cat that's going to get close to either of you with old Dwight around."

"Not that I don't appreciate the thought," I replied to Bill. "It's just that I'd feel better if neither Dwight nor some orange-coloured feline assassin were ever around for the rest of my life."

"That may be so," said Bill. "But seeing as that isn't going to happen, maybe we should make the best of things and have some dessert."

I sighed and rolled my eyes with frustration while Blackthorne and Big Bill Powell ordered strawberry shortcake with whipped cream and chocolate sauce. Not only did they seem undisturbed by the events of the day, they were laughing and exchanging witty comments like they were having the time of their lives.

I realised that even though both dogs were at opposite ends of the sometimes topsy-turvy culture of the city, they shared something in common: a love of adventure and excitement.

At the same time, the thought came to me that I had had just about all the adventure and excitement I needed to last me for the rest of my hopefully uneventful and tedious existence.

We stayed at the North Beach Fish House till well past midnight, Big Bill drinking beer, Blackthorne drinking espresso, and myself drinking steamed milk and tea.

As we were finally leaving I managed to get all the way to the street before I noticed that I had left my cane in the restaurant. I went back inside and after retrieving my walking stick, realised that my hip hadn't hurt for hours.

I shook my head and caught up to Blackthorne and Big Bill waiting outside.

26

THE NEXT MORNING, I came out of my bedroom to find Dwight Cruddles asleep on the floor of the living room. Blackthorne and I had tried to talk him out of staying with us, but he insisted that he was either going to sleep inside our apartment or outside in the hallway.

After some deliberation it was decided that Mrs Totts might think the worst if she found him asleep in the hallway. That, and the fact that it simply wasn't good manners to allow him to sleep out there, persuaded us to invite him in.

He was too large to stretch out on the small couch so I found him a pillow and some extra blankets, which he used to make a bed on the floor. I instructed him to make himself at home and left a small oil lamp burning so he could find the bathroom if he needed.

I had trouble sleeping at first. My life had been turned upside down. I was charged with murder and I had a bodyguard named Dwight sleeping outside my bedroom door. I couldn't help but wonder why I had ever associated with Samuel Blackthorne in the first place.

He sucked in trouble like a whirlpool sucks in floating debris. Individuals and events seemed to swirl around him, and anyone that got close was pulled in along with everything else.

I imagined what I would be doing if I hadn't met him that fateful night when I arrived in port. I would probably be living in a peaceful hotel or maybe a boarding house down by the wharf.

I'd be back to work because of the increased expense of living by myself. I'd probably be in bed early and up with the sun.

I'd have to work for one of the hospitals because

building a private practice would take too long. I'd probably fix my own meals in my room or eat at the counter in a café, by myself.

At least I'd be safe. At least my life would be predictable and orderly. I certainly wouldn't be dealing with criminals and counting machines and gamblers and thugs. I wouldn't be at risk of imprisonment, or pursued by killers, or staying out till all hours of the night.

Finally the sheer weight of exhaustion pulled me down into the dark recesses of unconsciousness.

When I awoke, I felt invigorated and refreshed, as if the horrible experiences I had suffered had not worn me down but made me stronger, more vital, more alive.

Dwight's eye opened when I walked by, and he stretched and sat up as I prepared some tea.

"Morning, Doc." He yawned. "How'd you sleep?"

"Not badly actually," I answered. "Quite well, now that I think about it. What about you?"

"Great."

"I still feel badly about you spending the night on the floor."

"No big deal," he replied as he stood and began to fold his blankets. "I sleep on the floor at home. Besides, you got a nice cosy place here. I don't mind it at all."

"Well, I certainly appreciate you looking out for Mr Blackthorne and me. It's a little awkward for me to get used to . . . your . . . protecting us. So I hope you understand if I appear rude."

"You've been very nice. Really. I know you don't want me around, but Bill said to make sure nothing happened to you or Mr Sam."

I was impressed by his easy demeanour and engaging personality, and although I disapproved of his presence, I couldn't help but begin to feel some fondness for the brown pit bull.

For most of the previous night he had seemed serious and distant. He often stood apart from us and hung back from any conversation, out of an intentional effort to recede into the background as well as a respect for our privacy and personal space.

Yet this morning he was talkative and cheerful. He neatly folded both blankets, and after fluffing the pillow, politely asked where he should put them.

I indicated the top shelf of the coat cupboard and finished placing a bag of fresh Earl Grey tea in a cup for each of us. The kettle began to whistle and I poured the boiling water into the porcelain containers.

There was a moment of silence while we each stirred our tea. I offered Dwight a bowl of sugar and he enthusiastically scooped out three heaping tea-spoonsful into his cup.

"Have you worked for Big Bill long?" I asked.

"About ten years," he answered. "Mr Powell took care of us when we got in some trouble and we've been with him ever since."

"He seems to ask a lot of you and your brothers."

"Yeah, that's true," he paused, thinking to him-self, "but he takes care of us, and I can't say that about anyone else."

"Well, he certainly knows how to have a good time."

"That he does," answered Dwight, smiling to himself.

Just then the front door opened and in stepped Blackthorne. His eyes were shining and he was breathing rapidly. He closed the door and produced a folded newspaper as he came into the sitting room.

"Gentlemen, we are going to a political rally tonight at the Palace Hotel. It seems a Mr Tilden Stubbs, business leader, city council member, and candidate for mayor, is addressing concerns about crime and other immoral behaviour."

"Why has Mr Stubbs suddenly sparked your interest?" I asked. "I thought you couldn't care less about politics or the affairs of government."

"Because if you study the photo of Mr Stubbs at a different rally a week ago, you will notice some of his aides standing behind him."

He handed me the folded newspaper and I examined the photo of a rather large bloodhound flanked by four other dogs and a cat.

Blackthorne began to recite a brief biography of Tilden Stubbs.

The outspoken political leader had made a fortune selling fire insurance to local businesses and then homes in the Bay Area. Some dogs said that if you didn't buy his insurance, you would soon find your building or home burned to the ground.

From there Stubbs began to buy warehouses near the wharf where he would charge ships to load, unload, and store their cargoes. According to Blackthorne it was rumoured that if a ship captain didn't use Stubbs' facilities and labourers, the cargo might sit on the dock for days. Fish would rot;

crates would get rained on, merchandise stolen. Ship captains learned quickly and pretty soon Stubbs controlled the docks.

Stubbs had risen in popularity by making fiery speeches about getting tough on criminals. He wanted more arrests and more prison time for a whole list of crimes. He wanted to issue licences to run casinos, and he wanted to stop any new casinos from being built. He wanted law and order and the voters ate it up.

As I listened to Blackthorne, I inspected the faces of the others in the photo, but could find nothing remarkable. I recognised no one.

Then I noticed something. The photo was black and white so it was impossible to tell what colour the cat was, but there was one other rather unique characteristic that showed clearly enough.

The cat standing behind Stubbs and to his left was missing an ear.

27

THAT NIGHT, AT 9:00 P.M. we found ourselves amid a crowd of several hundred angry citizens.

They were angry about taxes. They were angry about crime. They were angry about being angry.

They were listening to Tilden Stubbs talk about what was wrong with their lives.

He told them the government was stealing their money. They roared in agreement.

He told them that criminals were stealing their money. They roared in anger.

He told them that he could get their money back. They cheered for three solid minutes.

Tilden Stubbs was becoming a hero to the dogs of San Francisco. He told them who to blame for everything that was wrong in their lives. He told them why they should give him the power to fix things. He told them what they wanted to hear.

And they believed him.

Stubbs went on and on, barking out his plans for the future, hypnotising the crowd with every word, every gesture.

"He lays it on pretty thick, don't you think?" said Blackthorne as we watched Stubbs pounding his paw on the podium.

"I don't know," I replied. "It appears to be having the desired effect."

"What do you think, Dwight?" asked Blackthorne. "Do you follow politics?"

"I think he sounds like just about every other puffed up loud talker I've ever seen. They're so busy listening to the sound of their own voice, they forget to make sense, or they don't care."

"So you don't believe him?"

"I don't believe anyone who tells me they know what's good for me, unless it's my mama or Mr Powell."

Blackthorne made an expression of approval and began to make his way through the crowd. Dwight and I followed.

We were jostled around more and more as we went farther towards the front and the dogs pushed forward in an effort to be near Stubbs.

I felt slightly claustrophobic as the mob pressed closer. Blackthorne didn't seem to notice. Dwight didn't seem to care.

We got nearly to the front row, Blackthorne scuttling through the larger dogs' legs, myself following with a continuous stream of apologies as I picked my way past the hairy, shouting bodies.

Dwight was more direct. He pushed dogs out of the way without any hesitation or the slightest regret.

That's when I saw him: the apricot cat, the mysterious feline who always seemed to be lurking in the shadows. He was standing near the stage, in a roped-off area reserved for important friends and associates of Tilden Stubbs.

Suddenly the cat turned directly towards me and stared right at me, as if he knew who I was and wanted me to know that he knew. He reached up and scratched his head where his right ear should have been. His eyes moved from me and onto Blackthorne. Either I was imagining things or he had recognised us and seemed almost amused that we were there.

Blackthorne was motioning to Dwight and pointing at the cat, although I couldn't hear what he said above the roar of the crowd. He handed the pit bull something and Dwight put whatever it was in his mouth.

Some dogs were carrying signs that said things like: STUBBS FOR MAYOR! TRUST IN TILDEN! STUBBS MEANS BUSINESS!

Soon Dwight was winding his way through the crowd and moving closer and closer to the apricot cat. In spite of the red velvet rope that separated the cat and the crowd, the pit bull was able to get right next to him.

Dwight began to move his jaws in an exaggerated, earnest manner, and I realised Blackthorne had given him a large piece of chewing gum. Without any warning he suddenly reached into his mouth and pulled out the wad of gum. He leaned over the red velvet rope and in one motion stuck the sticky blob directly onto the fur of the one-eared cat.

The cat immediately twisted away and the gum stretched into a long strand as one part clung to the cat and the other remained in Dwight's paw. Security police formed a barrier between the crowd and the cat, and within seconds Dwight had faded into the swirling mob and was lost from sight.

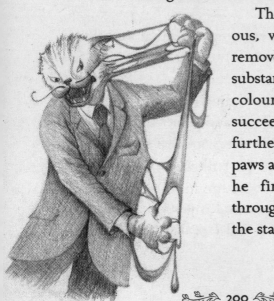

The cat, looking furious, was busy trying to remove the stringy, sticky substance from his apricot-coloured coat. He only succeeded in getting it further entangled in his paws and orange hair until he finally stormed out through a doorway behind the stage.

Blackthorne beckoned me to follow him, and we threaded our way through the swarm of Stubbs supporters. We met up with Dwight near the exit.

The three of us left the hotel and I filled my lungs with the cool, fresh air outside. I had always hated large crowds, and now I remembered why.

"Whatever were you trying to accomplish by sticking chewing gum into the fur of our one-eared feline friend?" I asked, bewildered. "I mean, I'm all for having a little fun, but don't you think we should take this thing a little bit more seriously?"

Blackthorne began to laugh and clapped me on the shoulder while he wiped a tear away with his other paw. "Sometimes, Smithfield, your sense of humour astounds me!"

I still had no idea what was so funny, and I made it clear that I wasn't amused by their childish antics.

When Blackthorne had finally stopped laughing, he removed a small vial from his pocket and motioned to Dwight, who produced the remaining part of the wad of chewing gum. The blob of gum was smaller now, since most of it was stuck to the cat, but what was left was completely covered with apricot-coloured fur.

Blackthorne carefully extracted several of the hairs and put them in the vial, which he then replaced in the front inside pocket of his green tweed jacket. He discarded the gum into a nearby rubbish bin, straightened his bow tie, and smoothed back his hair.

Then with a flourish, he signalled a cabbie and we set off into the foggy darkness.

28

THE NEXT MORNING, we were eating breakfast at Mrs Totts' kitchen when a tan, spotted boxer came through the door and walked directly up to our table. Dwight Cruddles stood up to confront him, but Blackthorne waved him back into his seat.

"It's all right, Dwight. I believe this chap has something for us."

It was then that I noticed the brown paper envelope in the boxer's paw. He bent down slightly and handed the envelope to Blackthorne.

"Excuse me, sir," said Blackthorne. "You obviously know my face, but I'm afraid I don't know you."

"I recognised you from your picture in the newspaper," answered the dog. "Front page!" He said it as if we should be proud of the distinction. "I'm just a messenger. Name's not important."

The boxer nodded his head in my direction. "You two are pretty famous. They told me if you weren't in your apartment, to look for you here."

"Thank you," said Blackthorne.

"Great," I complained sarcastically. "Now we're not only accused of being killers, everyone in town knows our faces!"

"Look at the bright side," said Dwight Cruddles. "From now on, dogs will think twice before they mess with you."

"Terrific," I moaned. "Now I can add *scary and threatening* to my list of accomplishments."

Blackthorne had opened the envelope and was reading its contents with a look of mild amusement on his face. He stroked his goatee a few times and looked up at the boxer with a twinkle in his eye.

"Tell Mr Stubbs we would be happy to attend.

There will be three of us." The boxer nodded, turned, and strode away without looking back.

Blackthorne handed me the manila card and cocked an eyebrow. "It seems that Mr Tilden P. Stubbs has asked us to lunch with him at his mansion on Nob Hill."

"What are we having?" asked Dwight Cruddles.

"It didn't say on the invitation, Dwight." Blackthorne winked. "But I can assure you it will be an interesting meal."

I looked at the card and checked my pocket watch. It was 9:43. In just over four hours, we would be having lunch with the dog responsible for a kidnapping, at least two murders, our arrest and imprisonment, the attempted murder of Big Bill Powell, and who knew what other evil deeds.

I swallowed hard and my mouth became dry. Somehow I didn't think I was going to have much of an appetite.

29

W E ARRIVED AT the mansion at two. An Irish setter in a butler's uniform opened the door and ushered us inside.

I had never been inside such a house, and despite my anxiety about being there, I was quite flabbergasted by the incredible display of wealth.

The entryway was covered entirely in alternating black and white squares of marble. A huge spiral staircase led to the upper rooms, and gold ornaments and fixtures sprouted from every surface.

The butler escorted us down the main hallway and into a large dining area that was near the back of the house. A large window along one wall provided a spectacular view of the city, the bay, and the open sea beyond.

As we entered the room the tall, imposing figure of a bloodhound came towards us from the opposite end. As he got closer his drooping jowls and sagging eyes tightened up with amusement and a smile came to his face.

"Tilden Stubbs." He reached out his paw and shook each of ours in turn, including that of Dwight Cruddles, who was still busy looking at the ornate carvings in the ceiling.

"Welcome to my home, gentlemen. I am so pleased you could come at such short notice."

"Thank you for having us," answered Blackthorne, also smiling.

"May I get you something to drink?"

"Coffee, please," said Blackthorne. I ordered an iced tea – my mouth was getting dry again – and Dwight Cruddles ordered a beer, but changed to a root beer after receiving a disapproving look from Blackthorne.

The butler went off to get our drinks, and Stubbs indicated that we sit down at one end of the large table.

"Gentlemen." He placed both paws on the table in front of him. "It has come to my attention that you have some suspicions about me and I'd like the opportunity to clear them up."

"By all means," said Blackthorne. "We would be most grateful if you would do that very thing."

Stubbs smiled that curiously soothing smile, the smile of a politician, and spoke to Blackthorne as if he were a child.

"I've heard about your hobbies, Mr Blackthorne, and I'm sure you are having a rousing time of it, playing your guessing games and your pretending. But this is the real thing and your little games are getting in my way. Do I make myself clear?"

The butler chose that moment to return with the refreshments, and everyone was silent while he carefully arranged four cloth napkins and placed the drinks on the table.

"If you are threatening me," answered Blackthorne quietly, "then you will have to be more specific. You see, the doctor and myself are in a compromising position with this murder charge and all that. It seems to me the only way we're going to clear our names is to prove who is the real killer."

He looked squarely at Stubbs for a split second. "Since that happens to be you, well, you can see the conflict."

"Very well," answered Stubbs, "but why should I care if you make accusations against me? It looks as though you are the one with the image problem."

"Let me give you the details," said Blackthorne, "and perhaps it will help resolve any doubts you might have."

Stubbs made a sweeping motion with his paw. "You have the floor, Mr Blackthorne. I'm anxious to hear your theories."

At this point I was beginning to wonder what Blackthorne was up to. He was offering to tell Stubbs everything he knew and Stubbs was accepting. If I didn't know better, I would say that Blackthorne was making some sort of deal.

I cursed Blackthorne's habit of keeping his plans to himself. After all, I was in this along with him and if he was going to give away everything we had found out to our worst enemy, at least he could have told me about it. But it was too late now, and I had no choice but to go along with him and find out later where it would eventually lead.

For the next thirty minutes Blackthorne spelled out his entire theory. Stubbs had wanted to take over virtually every gambling enterprise in the city and he had systematically run each of them out of business, one by one.

When they were nearly broke or the owner mysteriously died or disappeared, he bought them up at bargain prices, using a long list of fake names and phony companies so no one could trace them back to him.

The butler and two waiters served the salad. It was cold, crisp romaine lettuce with mandarin oranges and a tangy raspberry vinegar dressing.

After the waiters had left, Blackthorne continued.

Big Bill Powell was the last casino owner left and Stubbs knew he was either going to have to kill him or put him out of business. His first choice was to kill him, since he also owned the racetrack, which

Stubbs wanted even more than the casino, but the attempt failed.

The waiters, after removing the salad plates, served the main course: a lobster tail with a buttery, lemon-garlic sauce, asparagus, pineapple relish, and small purple potatoes.

Again Blackthorne waited silently until the waiters were finished. Only this time he carefully cut a small morsel of lobster and placed it in his mouth with the solid-gold fork. His eyes closed and he chewed slowly, savouring the flavour of the shellfish. Finally his eyes opened and he nodded his head at Stubbs with obvious approval.

"Magnificent lobster."

"Thank you so much," replied Stubbs. "I will have my chef give you the recipe for the sauce."

"I would appreciate that," said Blackthorne. He took another bite and chewed with obvious relish.

"Please continue," said Stubbs.

Blackthorne seemed to think a moment and then asked, "Where was I?"

"I believe you were accusing me of trying to murder Mr Powell."

"That's right," nodded Blackthorne, placing another forkful of lobster in his mouth. He went on to explain that, through his contacts, Stubbs learned of Patrick Kirkpatrick's invention and his involvement with Big Bill Powell. He decided to have Kirkpatrick shanghaied to keep Powell from getting the invention, and to keep Kirkpatrick where he could get him back in the future when he, Stubbs, eventually became the new owner of the racetrack.

"You're very thorough, aren't you?" asked Stubbs when Blackthorne paused to finish the last of his lobster.

"I'm not finished," replied Blackthorne. "When you discovered that Dr Smithfield and I were on the trail, you had us framed for the murder of your two kidnappers. You had to get rid of them anyway, so it was actually a convenient opportunity to make it look as if we had done it.

"The only problem," Blackthorne went on, "was that you sent the same cat to kill those two as you sent to kill Big Bill Powell.

"Big Bill didn't see his face, or for that matter, his missing ear, but he did see what colour he was: orange.

The same colour as the cat hair we found in Kirkpatrick's apartment and the same colour as the hair found on the bodies of the poor, dead kidnappers."

"Again, fascinating," said Stubbs, "but it proves nothing."

"Maybe," said Blackthorne. "But it is interesting that the orange cat hair found at the crime scenes also perfectly matches the colour and texture of one of your most trusted campaign workers."

"It is interesting indeed," came a voice from

behind us. Whoever it was had walked down the hallway and into the dining room without making any noise at all, as if he had appeared out of nowhere.

We all turned around, and there stood an apricot-coloured shorthaired cat, with only one ear.

"May I introduce Pierre Bouissard," said Stubbs as the cat bowed slightly and pulled up a chair. "I don't believe you've met."

"We haven't," replied Blackthorne, smiling and leaning forward to shake paws with Bouissard, "but I feel like I know you already."

"I, too, feel we have crossed paths before." The accent was silky and smooth. The cat smiled, showing two perfect rows of tiny, sharp teeth. "Perhaps in another life."

"Perhaps." Blackthorne smiled back, also showing his teeth.

"It took me an hour to get that gum out of my fur," purred the cat. There was a large bald patch on the side of his neck where the hair had been shaved.

"Sorry about that," apologised Dwight in a sarcastic tone. "Mr Sam wouldn't let me use my knife, so we came up with the gum thing."

The cat wrinkled up his nose with distaste. "I appreciate your consideration."

"Anytime," said Dwight.

"Now, now," said Stubbs, "we're not here to argue. We're here to come to an agreement."

That was when it hit me. We *were* here to make a

deal! Blackthorne was going to trade Stubbs information to let us go! He was giving up! I thought I had seen every kind of behaviour from Blackthorne, but I never thought he was a coward!

"Maybe *you* are here to come to an agreement!" I shouted at Stubbs. "And maybe *Blackthorne* is here to come to an agreement. But *my* silence is not for sale! I for one am going to take the stand and tell the court everything I know!"

Blackthorne made no expression and Dwight Cruddles watched with anticipation at what would happen next. He looked ready for anything.

Tilden Stubbs summoned the butler, who appeared with a box of cigars that he held out for everyone to select from. I declined, as did Blackthorne, but Dwight and Stubbs both lit up.

"Let me make it clear to you, Dr Smithfield," said Stubbs as he exhaled a cloud of blue smoke and shook out the wooden match. "What Mr Blackthorne obviously understands, and you do not, is that I will stop at nothing to accomplish my goals.

"For instance, let's say you were to begin shooting your mouth off to the newspapers, or the courtroom or whomever, that I was involved with this whole mess. Do you really think the police would arrest me?"

I didn't reply and he went on.

"It might cause public relations problems, of course, and no doubt interfere with my political plans. But I highly doubt anything more would come of it. It would, however, be an inconvenience, and since you have made it clear you are not for sale, I might have to resort to other means to keep you quiet."

My brow furrowed as I started to realise what he was getting at.

"Mrs Totts, for instance," said Stubbs. "It would be a shame if something horrible happened to her. I mean, what if there was an accident and her kitchen burned down? It might spread to your apartment, too. Now that would be a tragedy. She's such a kind old lady."

As I listened to Stubbs go on, it dawned on me how evil he really was. My lunch, as good as it was, felt as if it were going to come back up.

"Or maybe our Mr Kirkpatrick," continued

Stubbs. "Instead of being shanghaied, he might one night go for an evening swim and never come back. Imagine how heartbroken his sister, what was her name? Molly? Imagine how terrible she would feel to have found him and then lost him for a second time."

As Stubbs listed each of his horrible threats, he seemed to breathe more heavily and his eyelids began to droop, as if he was becoming drunk on his own wickedness.

Blackthorne remained silent, waiting for Stubbs to finish so we could get on with the business at hand. I now saw what Blackthorne had seen long ago. We were up against a monster that we would have to kill to be rid of.

"I know what you're thinking, doctor," said Stubbs, almost as if he had read my mind. "But you're not the type for violence. Think about it; you are a doctor. You've sworn to protect and save lives, not take them. You couldn't kill me if you tried."

"I could." It was Dwight Cruddles, speaking very quietly, and sounding very deadly.

"That's true, Mr Cruddles," said Stubbs. "But what would happen to your brothers? Jerry and Larry, is it?"

"Mike," answered Dwight with raw hatred in his voice. "Jerry and Mike."

"That's right," nodded Stubbs. "Jerry and Mike. Some night, they might just run into the wrong dog down at the bars on the wharf."

"Or cat," added the cat.

"He's right," agreed Stubbs. "Who else? Oh, yes, I almost forgot about that pesky dockworker. Max, is that his name? What would that big family of his do without a daddy? Seems like a high price to pay just to cause some trouble."

"Trouble?" I asked. "Murder, kidnapping, extortion, that's some pretty big trouble if you ask me."

"Do you really think anyone will believe you?" asked Stubbs. "You have some hair and some clever theories. So far I haven't seen any evidence that would convict me of anything. I might remind you, doctor, that you are the one charged with murder."

"What is your proposal?" asked Blackthorne, obviously fed up with the threats and counter threats.

"Simple," answered Stubbs. "I'll take care of things down at City Hall and your murder charges will be dropped. You two" – he looked at Dwight

Cruddles – "you *three* keep your mouths shut and nothing will happen to any of your friends."

"What about Big Bill Powell?" asked Dwight.

"Tell him I'm getting out of the gambling business, at least for now," said Stubbs. "It's too much trouble. I've found something better anyway. Construction. I'm thinking about building a bridge across the Golden Gate."

"That's all?" asked Blackthorne.

"That's all," answered Stubbs.

Blackthorne thought about it for a minute, and then his eyes became black as ink.

"Have you ever heard of a substance known as batrachotoxin?" he asked Stubbs.

"I don't believe I have," answered the bloodhound, "but I have no doubt that you are about to tell me."

"It is a poison," said Blackthorne. "The Choco tribe who live just west of the Andes mountains of Columbia produce it by scraping the oily secretions from the skin of a brilliant yellow tree frog known as *Phyllobates terribilis*."

"Fascinating," observed Stubbs. "As are all of your stories, my dear Blackthorne."

"A miniscule dose," continued Blackthorne, "roughly equivalent to a few grains of table salt, delivered to the victim on the surface of a tiny dart, will paralyze the lungs within fifteen seconds, the heart in thirty."

He fixed Stubbs with a piercing stare. "You will never see it coming. You will never hear it until it penetrates your skin. Once you realise what has happened, it will be too late."

"What is your point?" asked Stubbs, with mild amusement.

"My point," answered Blackthorne in a voice so low it could hardly be heard, "is that if anything happens to anyone I know, if anyone gets sick, if anyone loses his or her job, if anyone is hit by lightning. Anything."

Blackthorne got up from his chair.

"You will not live out the week."

"Thank you for your advice," said Stubbs in an unconcerned voice. "I will keep it in mind."

30

I DIDN'T SPEAK TO Blackthorne all the way home, and we didn't say much for the rest of the afternoon. I knew he had no other choice than to make a deal with Stubbs, but I was nevertheless feeling sorry for myself and angry that the bloodhound was getting away with murder.

We sent Dwight Cruddles home and read to ourselves for the remaining hours of daylight, each absorbed in his own thoughts.

At around 8:00 P.M. Blackthorne stood up and stretched. "What do you say we go out for dinner, Smithfield?"

"Is food the only thing you ever think about?" I asked, feeling irritated.

"You're not still upset about our arrangement with Stubbs, are you?"

"I can't help it," I replied. "It just seems so unfair!"

"Indeed it is," he agreed. "Maybe someday we'll get our chance for revenge, but until then I'm afraid he's got us. Unless we want to kill him, of course."

For a moment I couldn't believe what I was hearing. Could this be the reason Blackthorne didn't seem as upset over the whole thing as I was? Could he have been planning to kill Stubbs and his cat side-kick all along?

"You can't be serious?" I asked, not sure I wanted to hear the answer.

Blackthorne kept a straight face, and one eyebrow began to slowly rise as a look of wry menace crossed his bearded face.

"I guess we probably shouldn't," he said in a considering tone, as if he were giving it genuine thought.

After a moment he shook his head and his eyes widened as if he had come to his senses again. "How about the North Beach Fish House?" he asked, his mind returning to dinner.

"Fine," I answered, coming to the conclusion that truth and justice do not always triumph, no matter how much we wish it were so.

We finished dressing and caught a taxi to North Beach where we once more entered the hustle and bustle of the Fish House. We were led through the maze of dining rooms and hallways amid the sounds and smells of the familiar eating establishment, and I began to feel better.

Eventually we emerged in a private dining room, and I was surprised to see Big Bill Powell sitting at a large table with Dwight and the other two Cruddles brothers, Jerry and Mike.

Beside them sat Molly and Mrs Totts. On the other side sat Salvatore, Patrick Kirkpatrick, and Mrs Cardiccio.

We were warmly greeted by everyone around the table, and the waitress brought a milk for me and an iced coffee for Blackthorne. We sat down and ordered shrimp cocktail and oysters and crab cakes and stuffed mushrooms.

We spent the next few hours telling stories and laughing and eating and drinking. As the evening went on I found myself thinking about the agreement with Stubbs and how it was the only thing to do.

These dogs had become my friends, and they were far too important to risk.

It seemed that dogs like Stubbs were everywhere, and no matter how many were exposed, there were always more waiting to take their place.

I realised that only weeks earlier, I had arrived in the city with not a single friend and no ambition but to spend the rest of my life nursing my bad leg and avoiding any behaviour that might cause me anxiety or risk.

Now, as I looked at the smiling faces around the table, I felt a deep sense of happiness and belonging. For the first time in years I felt that I had finally come home to the friends I had always yearned for.

Big Bill was getting chummy with Mrs Totts, and Blackthorne was droning on about something or other with Molly Kirkpatrick. Salvatore was earnestly engaged in a conversation with the

Cruddles brothers, and Mrs Cardiccio had stuffed so much dessert in her mouth that small bits were flying out onto the front of Patrick Kirkpatrick as she told him about the ins and outs of the records department at City Hall.

I thought about the real story of Samuel Blackthorne and how the world should know of his keen intelligence and gift for solving the most complex of puzzles.

I had kept notes of our adventures in my journal, and it was at that moment that I vowed to somehow compile those writings in a way that would tell the public of the fascinating dog I had come to know as a true friend and intelligent and exciting companion.

Of course, I couldn't put this particular case to pen and paper, at least not for publication, but there would be another mystery and another puzzle to solve, and that one I would write about.

One day the world would know of the genius of Samuel Blackthorne, and then everyone would appreciate him the way I did.

Big Bill Powell started yelling at Blackthorne

about Mrs Totts and how she was the most charming creature he had ever set eyes on.

"How can I possibly repay you for bringing this goddess of elegance and grace into my dull and boring life?" he barked loudly, grabbing Blackthorne around his shoulders and pulling him close in a hug that could have crushed the smaller Blackthorne if Big Bill wasn't careful.

"You already have," replied Blackthorne.

"How's that?" asked Bill, his green eyes sparkling against his scruffy red hair.

"I told the waitress that you're paying for dinner."

Big Bill roared with laughter and raised his paw to get the waitress's attention.

"Another round for everybody," he yelled. "Another round for my friends!"

And as I looked around the table I realised there was no other place in the world that I would rather be than right here, with my friends.

That's when it hit me.

That's when I knew what I had to do.

31

TILDEN STUBBS WAS RIGHT. The police would never listen if we told about the murders, the kidnapping, the gambling casinos, the dog track, and the one-eared cat. Stubbs controlled too many individuals and had too much power to challenge directly.

But what if we went directly to the public?

What if we told the story in a way that the public would *want* to listen to?

I told the others of my idea.

After some skepticism it was agreed that the only way to keep Stubbs from one day changing his mind and deciding to kill one or all of us was to end his career once and for all.

But Blackthorne wasn't convinced.

"I don't think I want my personal experiences a matter of public knowledge," he said with a sneer.

"But we both know that to be safe from Stubbs, we must either ruin him or kill him," I pointed out.

Blackthorne did not reply right away. Instead he looked around the table, inspecting the faces of each individual, weighing his decision.

"Killing him would be the most reliable."

Big Bill looked pleasantly surprised at Blackthorne's statement. "Now that is the smartest thing you've said all night."

"You aren't serious?" I pleaded. "That would make us as bad as Stubbs. Besides, we'd still have the cat to deal with."

"We could kill them both," said Dwight Cruddles. His brothers nodded in agreement.

"Smithfield's right," said Blackthorne finally. "Violence should always be avoided if there is a satisfactory alternative. It is nearly always the least intelligent option."

"Then you'll agree to go along?"

"Fine," answered Blackthorne. "I'll go along."

"I will give you first approval on every page," I assured him. "If there are any inaccuracies or you don't like the way you're being portrayed, you are free to make any corrections or deletions."

"I'm sure your descriptions will be most satisfactory."

"If I might make a suggestion," said Big Bill. "There will be a period of time after the story is made public when Tilden Stubbs is going to be quite angry. There is no telling what he will do, and I suggest that all of us consider taking a holiday for a few weeks while matters take their course."

"I don't know about anyone else," said Patrick Kirkpatrick, "but I can't afford to take a holiday."

"Me neither," agreed Mrs Cardiccio.

"Tell you what," said Big Bill. "I have a yacht that I like to take down the coast around this time of year to get a little sun and relaxation. It sleeps a few dozen, and aside from the crew, most of the cabins are usually empty. Why don't all of you spend a month in some warmer waters with me? The whole thing would be at my

The Adventures of Samuel Blackthorne

expense, of course. I've got more money than I know what to do with and I'd love to have the company."

"I don't take charity," said Mrs Cardiccio.

"It's not charity," laughed Big Bill. "I nearly lost my livelihood when Stubbs tried to take over my territory. If it wasn't for you folks, I might be dead broke right now, or worse. I would be honoured if you would allow me this small token of appreciation."

"It would certainly be safer if no one was in the vicinity when that story gets out," observed Blackthorne.

"As for Patrick," said Big Bill, "you're going to be very rich one day, my friend. I'll advance you some money on your invention and you can quit your job.

"Molly, you're graduating soon anyway. It's time to take a break before you start your medical career."

Big Bill looked at Mrs Cardiccio. "I imagine you've built up quite a lot of holiday time that you've never taken. Am I right?"

Mrs Cardiccio squirmed in her chair. "Well, I haven't really had anywhere to go, until now."

"Then it's agreed," barked Big Bill.

And it was.

32

S O I BEGAN TO WRITE. I carefully reconstructed every event. I edited and rewrote passages from my notebooks. I double-checked my facts. I read and reread my manuscript.

It took nearly a month, but eventually I was satisfied.

I submitted the first few installments of *The Adventures of Mr Samuel Blackthorne* to the editors of the newspaper on the day before we set sail, and they immediately agreed to run them. I received twenty-five dollars along with a promise to buy additional chapters as soon as they became available.

When the paper hit the streets, the story was received with enthusiasm and quickly became the talk of the town. As each episode came out the readership grew, and soon the public began clamouring for an investigation.

Despite initial denials, Stubbs became the target of a number of political and then criminal inquiries. His career began to spiral down and first his cronies, then his flunkies, began to desert him one by one.

Eventually the city prosecutors brought charges against him, but Stubbs, along with his one-eared sidekick, disappeared before they could be arrested. I suspect we will never hear from either of them ever again.

Meanwhile we sailed to San Diego and then continued down to Mexico where we spent our days in the sun and our nights under the stars, trading stories and eating a most wonderful and ever-changing menu of culinary delights that Big Bill's personal chef, Santiago, created on a continual basis.

It was at the same time a relaxing and exhilarating experience as I was able to learn ever more fascinating things about each of my newfound friends.

Big Bill had chartered his yacht for a fishing expedition upon our return to San Francisco, and after six weeks at sea, everyone prepared to go back to their normal lives.

As it happened, however, the group who had reserved the vessel, having read of our exploits, invited Blackthorne and myself to accompany them on the journey. Since neither of us had been to Alaska, and we had no pressing business, we accepted the generous offer and decided to stay on for the trip.

We required a few days at the docks to restock and refit the ship for its new destination. Blackthorne and I said our good-byes to Bill, Dwight, Patrick, and the others, collected our mail, and spent two evenings back in the old digs before returning to the ship for our departure.

We left the bay through the Golden Gate and began our journey to the colder climes of the North. Once again we were in the capable paws of the quiet and somewhat mysterious Captain Dan and his steady crew.

Our destination was Prince William Sound, Alaska, the home of the Pacific halibut.

From birth the halibut always swims with its left side down and its right side up. Before the creature is six months old, the left eye actually migrates around the skull until both eyes are on the right side of its head, the side that perpetually points towards the surface.

Feeding on tiny crustaceans and smaller fish in the rich, icy waters of the Gulf of Alaska, the strange beast can grow to a length of eight feet and a weight exceeding four hundred pounds.

In Middle English its name derives from the fact that it could only be eaten on holy days. It was the *holy fish* or the *haly-butte*, and as neither Blackthorne nor myself had ever had the experience of catching one of these giants of the deep, we felt it was too good of a chance to pass up.

The expedition was not only a success – we managed to bring in several of the massive and extremely odd-looking brutes – but it was also an experience that would require several dozen more pages if I were to tell it here.

So I won't, as it is off the subject.

It has taken us an additional three months, but the voyage was well worth it and we are now on our way home, which we expect to reach within the week.

Awaiting us when we stopped in port in Vancouver was a letter from Molly Kirkpatrick, and I enjoyed catching up on the news of what's happened since our friends departed ship.

Molly is in residence at Children's Hospital in San Francisco, and although she's working the exhausting schedule of all young doctors-in-training, she's finding the experience both challenging and rewarding.

Her brother Patrick is busy working on perfecting the design of the counting machine, as well as a method to connect several of them together. Big Bill is already counting the money he will make when the machines are put to use.

The Cruddles brothers are managing one of Bill's twenty-four-hour casinos. They each work a different eight-hour shift, so one of them is always there.

Since none of the patrons ever see any of the three together at the same time, it has become common opinion that the same casino manager is always on duty, night or day, seven days a week.

Big Bill and Mrs Totts are apparently an item, but Mrs Totts continues to open her kitchen at 6:00 A.M. every morning as she has for the past twenty-two years. She won't accept a penny from Big Bill, and even refuses his gifts. She says it would change their relationship, and she likes it just the way it is.

Mrs Cardiccio returned to City Hall after her well-deserved holiday, and Salvatore started a part-time position as a doorman and bouncer at the Palace Hotel.

All in all, everyone is doing well and I am anxious to see them and return to my work and a normal daily schedule.

I realise, however, that my life will never truly be normal again. I have been changed forever by the events and experiences of the last few months, but most of all by the power of Blackthorne's amazing intellect and charismatic personality.

Often, late at night, after the moon had set and the Milky Way shone overhead, we would stand at the stern of the ship, and Blackthorne would begin to sing in a high, clear voice. He would sing Celtic songs, their ancient melodies and indecipherable lyrics evoking a haunting wistfulness that pulled at the core of my being.

Although medicine will always be my calling, I have enjoyed my first experience as a writer, and I look forward to the next adventure with eagerness, anticipation and, I must admit, just a touch of nervousness.

Now, as I sit here on the deck of this fine vessel, I am amazed at the fabulous twists and turns my life has taken since meeting that small package of ingenuity and daring by the name of Samuel Blackthorne.

I can only wonder where he will take me next.

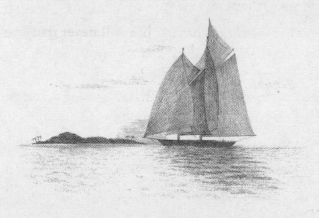

Scott Emerson has been a dog lover all his life. A former resident of San Francisco, he now lives in Phoenix with his wife, Molly; his daughters Kahley and Rainey; and, of course, his dogs and faithful companions, Sam and Ed.

Viv Mullett is a graphic designer, illustrator and painter. She lives in Wales.